Doppel Paladin

The Mya Yu Series

Lera Bishop

This book is dedicated to my youngest son, Liam. He's been such a light during the darkest times of my life. And I'm hoping that me pursuing my dreams will encourage him to do the same. Sky's the limit!

Contents

Chapter 1...1

Chapter 2... 13

Chapter 3... 27

Chapter 4... 38

Chapter 5... 57

Chapter 6... 70

Chapter 7... 79

Chapter 8... 88

Chapter 9... 97

Chapter 10 103

Chapter 11 114

Chapter 12 123

Chapter 13 129

Chapter 14 144

Chapter 15 153

Chapter 16 164

Chapter 17 170

Chapter 18 181

Chapter 19 186

Chapter 20 194

Chapter 21 207

Chapter 22 220

Chapter 23 231

Chapter 1

In the beginning, I had no understanding of who or what I truly was. I was just like everyone else, living a life planned out down to the minute. Everything seemed predictable, stable even. But one day, it all changed. The world I thought I knew was no longer the same, and everything I once believed to be certain began to unravel.

It was a world divided into three syndicates, the Syphoners, Pacifists and Agros. Each of these groups needed me for different reasons—some for noble purposes, others for…well, less honorable ones. I found myself caught in a relentless tug-of-war, trying to help both the Pacifists and the Agros get what they desired. But as you can imagine, our approaches to dealing with the enemy couldn't have been more different. The clash of ideologies was inevitable. Were there bumps along the way? Of course! How do you possibly accommodate two different groups that operate on opposite ends of the spectrum? The endless impossibilities that stared me in the face at times were too much to endure. I often found myself on the verge of giving up, yearning to escape back to my "normal and happy" life, the one I thought was so simple and carefree. I did my best to please everyone, to help them reach their goals, all the while forgetting about the one person who stared back at me in the mirror. Who was there to help me? The pressure was relentless. and I began to realize something—I'd always thought people were complex, but I was wrong. There was no instruction manual on this planet that could have possibly prepared me for this. Through it all, I couldn't help but wonder: Who was I really becoming in the midst of it all? My name is Mya Yu, and this is my story...

***

The smell of smoke fills my nostrils. Where am I, and how did I get here? There are flames everywhere. Men and women crawl across the floor, desperate to escape the fumes. The entire town is on fire, and no one seems to be spared. I hear the crackling and popping sounds from the blaze, and the smoke tightens around my throat, making it hard to breathe. I don't remember anything or anyone in this city, yet anger surges through me, overwhelming and unshakable. It feels like fury is pouring out of my skin, feeding the fire. Sweat trickles down my face, the heat pressing in on all sides. The flames twist and leap as children run, screaming, some engulfed in the blaze. I see people I vaguely recognize, but for the life of me, I can't remember where from. Chaos is all around me, but one question keeps echoing in my mind: where am I, and why am I here?

***

"Mya, wake up! Wake up!" whispered my roommate, Noreen, as she nervously tapped my shoulder. "You're having a bad dream, and you were talking in your sleep... again."

2

In a daze, I sat up in my bed and grabbed my cell phone to check the time; it was 2 A.M. I reached for a small towel from my bedside table, wiped my wet face and pulled my damp t-shirt that clung to my clammy skin.

"You kept saying something about a fire," Noreen pressed, wiping sleep from her brown eyes and fixing her silk head wrap over her frizzy red hair. "You want to tell me what all that was about?" she asked.

"Uh… maybe another night. You should go back to sleep," I said, hoping she would drop the subject.

Noreen walked across the hall from my room to the kitchen to get me a bottle of water, which I guzzled half without taking a breath.

"You sure? You know I'm a good listener," Noreen probed.

"Yeah, I know. I'm okay, though," I said, wiping water from my lips. From the look on Noreen's face, I knew she wasn't buying my story. "Go back to bed. I'm fine. I promise," I assured her.

"All right, well, you know where to find me if you need me," Noreen said, walking back to her room. "Goodnight."

"Night and thanks, Nor."

I quickly changed my clothes and lay back down in bed, uncertain what my nightmare meant. For the past few months, I've had recurring dreams, and I'm not sure why. Before I had the chance to analyze my thoughts any further, my eyelids became heavy, and I was gone again.

I gasped for air as I shot up in my bed and right away checked the time: 8 A.M. It took a moment for me to register that it was, in fact, Monday morning, and my first class started... well, right then. I sprinted to the bathroom, took the fastest shower possible, heaved my curly mane into a ponytail puff, grabbed my bag and books, had breakfast to go and was out the door.

Class was in session and every student was fixated on the professor speaking at the front of the class. I tiptoed to an empty seat at the back of the room, trying my best not to make a sound. Of course, nothing gets past my law and ethics professor, Mr. Henry.

"Well, thanks for finally joining us, Ms. Yu," he acknowledged. As if on cue, all my classmates turned to stare at me.

I always wondered why people did that as if they've never seen me before. Are they trying to make a statement, or could they all be *that* meddlesome? I wish they would all just turn around and stop brown-nosing.

At that moment, every student turned back around and faced forward simultaneously. Very weird!

"Sorry, sir. It won't happen again," I reply quietly.

I pulled out my textbook, pens and notebook while trying to get my mind into journalism mode. I discovered my love for writing when I was 13 years old while living with my adoptive parents, Veronica and James. That year was the most difficult year of my life and writing was the only way I was able to express myself and feel like I didn't have to pretend to be this happy preteen that everyone wanted me to be. They were great people and did the best they could, but no one could possibly understand the frustration of not being able to recall my past—where I came from, my birth parents… any of it. It was like my memory had vanished from my mind. The doctor had said that after the car accident, it would take some time for my memories to come back, but it had been years, and still nothing. So there I was, pursuing my dream of becoming the next Alice Walker. Except my body was present, but my brain was elsewhere. The dream—or nightmare, for lack of a better word— pulled me in once again, as vivid and unsettling as ever.

***

Class is over, and I'm rushing through the hall to get to my next class. The hallway is always packed, no matter what time of day it is. I can hear everyone chatting about their plans for the weekend and who's going to which party. I glance up at the huge clock on the wall in the hallway: 10 A.M. I have a few minutes before my class starts. Not paying attention to where I'm going, I suddenly turn and bump into a girl I've never met before, sending my books tumbling to the floor.

She bends down, picks them up, and hands them to me with a smile.
"Make sure to watch where you're going next time. Here you go," she says.

I give her a polite smile. Obviously, I know I need to watch where I'm going, I think to myself. Her olive skin and light brown eyes complement each other perfectly. Her shoulder-length wavy hair looks effortless, as though not a single strand is out of place. She's wearing loose-fitting jeans, a long-sleeved black shirt, and a beautifully patterned scarf around her neck. As she hands me my books, I notice the intricate designs on her hands.

"Thanks," I say, my gaze lingering on her henna. "I like your henna. I'm Mya... I guess I'll see you around," I call out as I quicken my pace to get to my next class on time.

"I know who you are," she calls back with a playful tone. "See ya!"

I turn slightly, unsure if I heard her right, but she's already walking away with her friend. I don't get a good look at her friend, only catching the bright yellow backpack decorated with a sea of buttons before they disappear down the hall.

***

"Ms. Yu? MS. YU!" I heard as I snapped out of it, the person beside me cleared his throat and nudged me with his elbow. "I asked a question, and I'm waiting on the answer," Mr. Henry said, looking at me suspiciously with his head tilted to one side.

I heard my peers whispering, wondering what was going on with me. Mr. Henry kept his gaze on me. I looked around, screaming for help with my eyes.

"Sorry, I didn't hear your question. What was it again?" I could feel myself getting warm with embarrassment. Thankfully, another student gave me a hand and answered the question before it went any further. Perhaps she heard my cries for help.

"The purpose of the code of ethics is to govern behaviours of members and to increase the level of competence and standards of care within the group," the girl blurted out, glancing back at me.

Thank you, I mouthed to her, and she nodded and smiled.

"Thank you, Ms. Medina and Ms. Yu. Can you see me after class, please?"

For the remaining 15 minutes of class, my mind was swarming with questions I couldn't answer myself. What is happening to me? I legitimately thought I was in the hall speaking to that girl. It felt so real, yet I was here in class the whole time.

Class was finally over, for real this time, so I grabbed my possessions and dragged my feet to Mr. Henry's desk. I was not in the mood for a lecture. I figured if I admitted my wrongdoings first, it would cut what he had to say to me by at least half.

"Mya, I…"

"Sorry to cut you off, Mr. Henry. I just wanted you to know I take full responsibility for my actions and lack of participation in class today. I promise from this day forward, I will do my best to keep focused in class." Not noticing, I blurted everything all at once I took a deep breath once I finished.

"Is that all?"

"Yes."

"Good! I was just going to ask if you're all right because…" he sighed as he pulled out a few sheets of paper from his briefcase. "I gave back these tests when class started, and I wanted to speak to you about yours."

I peer down at the test covered in red ink and notes of corrections. Funny enough, I actually thought I did well on that test, at the time anyway.

"I see… I'll do better," I say nonchalantly.

"Good… but be advised that you have almost two months left of the year. You started the year off so strong so I find it strange you'd switch so quickly. Is there something you're not telling me?"

"Nope," I lied. "But I appreciate your concern, Mr. Henry. Are you always this involved with your students?"

"I step in when necessary. You know where my office is if you ever need to talk."

"Great. I'll keep that in mind," I answered, darting for the door. I didn't want to be late for my next class.

I watched Mya as she rushed out of my class… I see my daughter when I look at her. They are similar in a lot of ways… mostly with the attitude. I miss her dearly, but since she passed, I have nothing left to live for … nothing left to look forward to. My wife left me once she saw the transformation I'd made… she said she couldn't condone what I was doing, but she'd always love me. She wouldn't love me if she knew me now. The Ian Henry she married is dead, and a new man was birthed. We Syphoners aren't liked within our world. The Agros want us dead… the Pacifists want us stopped. But if people were just more open-minded and allowed themselves to be… free… allowed themselves to simply live… then maybe they would understand that we aren't thieves, but this IS how we should be. It's not something I wanted for my life… but now that it's happened, I embrace it wholeheartedly.

Leaving the class, I stepped into a hallway swarming with pupils hustling to their next class. I watched as the different cliques chattered away about their weekend plans while making their way through the hallway. There were the techies, whom I loved… they're always available when I need their help. There were the jocks, the loners, the anime junkies, the artsy types, the pep squad, and then there's me. I personally don't like to categorize myself with any group because I'm friendly to everyone no matter what age, gender or group they associate with. I guess that would make a nomad. Create my own clique.

I make my way through the corridor, smiling and waving at those who saw me. I glanced at the clock to check the time: 10 A.M. I paused as the déjà vu feeling started to set in. I turned the corner with my books in hand and bumped into a girl dropping all my belongings on the floor. Before me stood the exact same girl I saw in my vision. Everything was the same, right down to the clothes she was wearing.

"Sorry about that. Make sure to watch…"

"Where I'm going next time?" I say, cutting her off while staring at her bewildered. "Yea…I know." I immediately bent down and gathered my things when I noticed the henna designs on her hands. I nearly dropped my books again.

"Nice design," I spluttered, observing her. I have to get out of here. What is going on? I backed away and headed towards the exit.

"I'm Mya, but you already knew that, didn't you?" I say.

"I'm Zohrah, and yea, I did. Are you okay? You look pale."

I couldn't get out of the building fast enough, but before I left, I took one last peek behind me and Zohrah was looking at me just as puzzled as I felt. I ran to the bus stop to catch a ride home.

I stood waiting for the bus to arrive in silence as I dissected the events of what happened back at school. Questions kept popping into my head like, who was that girl… Zohrah? Why was she in my vision? The only thing I knew for sure was something was happening to me, I just couldn't put my finger on exactly what it was.

"Hey, it's Mya, right?" I heard a voice say from behind, startling me. I turned around to see who it was and it was the same girl from my class who saved my life.

"Yep, that's me. Thanks for helping me back there. I guess I blanked out for a bit," I said.

"It's totally cool. That class is so boring, it's remarkable that people stay awake at all. You may want my notes, though; today, we took some pretty important ones that may be on a test later on," she said while twirling her jet-black curls around her acrylic nails.

She wore dark denim jeans with a long sleeve crop sweater showing a bit of her midriff with a leather jacket over top. She was all around an attractive girl, and I think she knew it.

"Aw, man! Thanks, I didn't even think about that. My mind is all over the place. Put your number in my phone, and I'll meet you later for the notes," I said passing her my phone. My bus arrived just as she finished, and I glanced down to see the name in my phone. "Thanks, Sophia. I'll text you later or something."

"Bye!"

Chapter 2

I'm not the type of person to tell anyone my business; I pretty much stick to myself and I believe it's better that way. Since moving out, two and a half years ago, Noreen has been the most consistent person in my life. I have next to no memory of my real parents or my life prior to being 11 years old, for that matter.

Three years ago

No one dared to speak above a whisper in the City Hall Public Library. The only sound I could hear was fingers clicking against the keyboards as students surfed the web and researched for school assignments. I, for one, was on a different quest: apartment hunting. I've been living with a girl who I thought was cool until I realized she had a real knack for getting under my skin and sticking her nose in places it didn't belong. The last time I discovered she had gone through my room and stolen a few of my personal possessions, and that was the last straw for me. I had every newspaper in front of me, as well as my laptop, open on different sites advertising places for rent. My biggest issue was the nice apartments were always the most expensive, and I refused to dwell in a bedbug or roach infested place. Just the thought made me cringe. However, I have been on the hunt for over a week and still nothing.

A young woman with silk-pressed, shoulder-length red hair slid into the chair in front of me, drinking a green smoothie. Her yoga pants, tank top and Nike shoes indicated she either just came from a workout or she enjoyed wearing active gear for sport. Judging by the smooth, freshly done hair, I'll assume the latter. She slurped her drink loudly and slammed her heavy backpack on the table. I looked up for a moment, and she gave me a half smile. She peeked over her backpack to all the newspapers spread out in front of me.

"You looking for a place?" she asked curiously.

"Yea. No luck, though," I replied, writing down a superintendent's number to call later.

"Yea, finding a nice apartment isn't easy," she said, gulping her beverage.

"Yep," I answered with my eyes glued to the paper.

"What if I told you I know of a place that is reasonably priced and spacious," she queried, placing her drink down on the table and leaning in so only I could hear her.

I looked up at her instantly.

"I'm listening."

"Well, my roommate just moved out last week, and I need someone. You interested?" she asked eagerly. Then she held her hand out to me. "I'm Noreen."

We sat there and spoke for hours about the apartment. She took me to see it that same day, and I was moved in a week later.

Present

From the outside looking in, Noreen looks very plain Jane, but within her simplicity, there's a beauty that requires no adjustments. I always told her she reminded me of a Zoe Kravitz minus the red carpet glam. Not to mention her personality, something about her just makes you want to spill your deepest and darkest secrets. Although I have not told anyone about my blurry past or annoying nightmares, I needed to vent to someone about my déjà vu episode, and Noreen was the only person I felt I could trust.

"Hey Nor! Nor you home?"

"I'm in my room! Coming!" she sang. "What's up?" she asked as she walked into our living room, where I was pacing back and forth. "Oh boy, what happened now?"

Noreen sat on the couch and listened to me go through my day as I explained to her in detail what happened. I decided it would be best to omit my dream, which may be a lot to digest on top of everything else I was telling her.

"Do you think I'm crazy?" I asked, looking at her, hoping she would tell me what I wanted to hear, not what I needed to hear.

"Of course not! Listen, you are NOT crazy! Okay! You just had a SERIOUS case of déjà vu. I'm sure it happens to other people… somewhere. You just need a good night's rest and to start again from scratch tomorrow," Noreen said, pouring me a glass of Moscato. "But sleep will have to wait because tonight we are going out! Don't act like you forgot."

"Huh? What are you talking about?" I asked, trying to act like I didn't remember what she was referring to; my acting skills are certainly not up to par. "Fiiiiiine! Yes, I remember. I was hoping no one else would. Do we have to go out? I'm not really into it this year."

"Mya, don't be silly. We're going out, and we're leaving here at nine tonight. Oh, and try putting some effort into your outfit, please, your birthday only comes once a year," Noreen said, as her eyes slowly observed me from head to toe as if to signify that what I was currently wearing was not birthday attire. Once her point was made, she turned on her heels and marched back to her room.

"Whatever. I'll be ready for nine," I said, going into my bedroom and closing the door behind me.

My birthday shindig was hours away, in the meantime, I thought I should get notes from the girl in my class so I can read them this weekend and get caught up. I got my phone from my jacket pocket and sent Sophia a text message. She responded right away and agreed to meet close to where I lived.

I walked into my favourite coffee shop around the corner from me; I arrived first with my laptop in hand. As I opened the door, the aroma of pastries and flavoured hot chocolates filled my nostrils. It was quiet tonight; just a few people sat down talking amongst each other. I could hear sizzling grilled cheese and Panini sandwiches as the owner's son, Johnny, placed them on the griddle. I loved coming here because of the warm welcome I always received. They make you feel like family here.

"Hey, Mya. You having the usual today?" Johnny asked with his heavy Italian accent while smiling ear to ear. I love that he remembers my order.

"Hey, Johnny," I smiled back. "Just my hot chocolate today. I already ate."

"Already ate! Next time, then, uh? Hot chocolate coming right up!"

Once my order was ready, I grabbed a seat and took a few sips, allowing the hot chocolate to warm me up from the crisp fall air as I waited for Sophia. Moments later, she arrived. As she walked into the coffee shop, every male in there was at her command. I rolled my eyes, wondering what I'd gotten myself into.

"Hey!" she said bubbly as she sat down across from me. "Here are my notes. I'm going to grab a coffee."

I start typing franticly so I can finish as soon as possible. I already know I have absolutely nothing in common with her. She sat back down, holding her steaming cup and looking around the coffee shop. I stared at the computer screen, hoping she would take the hint and do something else so we wouldn't have to converse.

"So! You come here often?" Sophia asked, blowing on her hot beverage to cool it down. I need to get better at dropping hints.

"Often enough," I replied flatly.

"Oh! Any plans tonight?" she asked. Evidently, she was eager to make conversation. I'll play along. A wise person once told me not to judge a book by its cover… and by a wise person, I mean Noreen.

"It's my birthday today, so my roommate is forcing me to get some drinks and food. Nothing too crazy."

"Oh my gosh! Happy birthday! Sounds super fun. How old are you turning?"

"20," I reply.

"My 19th birthday was last month, and my friends threw me this huuuuge surprise party. It was epic," Sophia smiled as she reminisced.

I quickly smiled back and continued typing, determined to finish.

"Any idea where you're planning to go?" she asked.

"Nope. My roommate is doing the planning."

I resumed typing my notes while Sophia stared in my direction. I knew what she was waiting for, part of me was trying to avoid it, but the other part of me couldn't shake the feeling that she was supposed to come with us. I usually try my best to go with my gut.

"Did you… want to come?" I muttered. "It will just be…."

"Of course, I'd love to come! Should I dress up or is it a casual thing? I mean you should dress up because it is your birthday. It's okay, I'll find something to wear. Did you guys need a ride? I can pick you guys up… what time were you planning to go? Who's else is going?" she inquired, looking excited.

"It's just my roommate Noreen and myself and we're planning to be ready for nine," I answered while closing my laptop.

"Perfect! Nine it is."

I thanked Sophia for agreeing to meet me and sharing her notes and walked back home to relax and mentally prepare for later on. I gave Sophia my address, and we said our goodbyes.

Back in my room I searched through my closet looking for something to wear. I wanted to be comfortable and sexy at the same time. I settled on a black dress I bought a few months ago but didn't have the chance to wear yet. The dress was had long sleeves and was backless, showing my rich melanin complexion. It really took me out of my comfort zone. The contour, form-fitting dress accentuated my curves. I'm not the best at walking in heels, however, I wouldn't hear the end of it from Noreen if I tried anything BUT heels with this dress. I finished my make up and was putting the last finishing touch to my edges and ponytail puff when I heard a knock at our front door. From the sound of the commotion, I knew Sophia arrived. I double-checked myself in the mirror, moisturized the important areas, and then walked out to the living room, trying my best not to fall flat on my face. Noreen and Sophia stopped in their tracks once I was in clear view.

"You look amazing, Mya!" Sophia said.

"Yea you clean up real nice," Noreen confirmed.

"Thanks, guys. Hopefully, I can last tonight in these shoes," I said, holding one leg out and showing them off.

Some hours later, after a few glasses of wine, champagne and a full stomach, Noreen and Sophia practically forced me to go to a nightclub. Fortunately for them, with a few drinks in my system, it doesn't take much convincing to get me to go along with their plan.

"You are going to have so much fun. And if in an hour you aren't enjoying yourself, we can leave, deal?" Sophia negotiated.

"Deal," I replied.

We arrived at Club 6IX in the downtown district. I could feel the vibrations of the music from the outside of the building. The streets were buzzing with people dressed to impress, deciding where to go next. As we turned the corner, we saw the lineup going down the street to get inside the club.

"There's no way we will get inside tonight," groaned Noreen.

"I have a friend who works security. Let's walk to the front and see if he's working," Sophia said as she sashayed ahead putting more sway in her hips as she walked.

We strolled to the front of the line, trying to see who was working the doors. I see Sophia asking a man for her friend Andy. Noreen is trying to peek beyond the crowd to see what was going on inside. I stood observing everyone while the cool wind blew around my bare legs, giving me the chills. I couldn't help but wish to myself that we were inside enjoying the music and not out here in the cold.

"Hey," one of the security officer tapped my shoulder, and I turned around. "You looking to get in?"

Sophia ran over to me and answered before I had the chance.

"Uh yea! Today is her birthday!," Sophia said, pointing at me.

"This way!" the security officer said while leading the way through the angry crowd. People yelled how unfair it was as we passed by them standing in line.

Noreen, Sophia and I exchanged glances as we took him up on his offer.

"It's like he read my mind," I whispered to Noreen.

"Are you complaining?" she asked.

"Hell no! Let's go!" I smirked.

Inside 6IX Night Club was dark for a moment, then shots of bright florescent lights flickered along the ceiling and walls, bringing the place to life. People all around danced and sang along to the songs they knew. The bar was flooded with people buying drinks. A pair of male hands wrapped around my waist, surprising me.

"Dance with me," he said softly with his face close to my neck inhaling my perfume.

"Maybe next time," I said, squirming from his grasp and smiling awkwardly. He winked and turned around, looking for his next victim.

With a sigh of relief, I turned towards Sophia, who was already walking ahead of me to the bar. I looked to my right to see Noreen already on the dance floor with some guy. I decide to follow Sophia to the bar.

Two hours later of non-stop dancing and probably making a fool of ourselves, we were sweating from head to toe.

"I'm so hot," Sophia said, fanning herself with her hands. "Follow me outside for a minute to get some fresh air."

"Sure," I said, feeling hot myself. I turned and asked Noreen if she wanted to join us. She said she needed to go to the bathroom instead, so we agreed to meet back there in 15 minutes.

Sophia led the way through the crowd and to the back of the club, where the emergency doors were. She cracked it open a bit to let some air in. I opened the door more so I could feel the breeze as well. In the distance, I noticed a man standing further down the dimly lit alleyway, looking around like he was expecting someone.

"Doesn't that look like Mr. Henry?" Sophia asked, squinting her eyes.

"It does look like him," I said, ducking down so he couldn't see us properly. There's nothing worse than seeing your teacher out of school and having to make small talk. I took my phone out of my clutch to check the time, 1:56 A.M.

"Isn't it weird for him to be out here at this time… I mean, he's a teacher! Gross!" Sophia whispered, shivering.

"It's definitely weird that he's in an alley at 2 am," I replied.

"You know we have no business spying on Mr. Henry like this, right?" Sophia pointed out as she checked her make up with her compact mirror. "You know what people say, curiosity killed the cat," she said, smacking her lips together reapplying her lip-gloss.

"Well, it's a good thing we aren't cats then," I said, smiling, taking one heel off to keep the door ajar. We crouched behind a near by dumpster to get a better view and possibly hear what was to be said.

"This is a waste of time!" Sophia whispered. "And it stinks out here, let's go back!"

"Fine, let's go," I reply reluctantly.

Just as we were about to head back, three others joined him. One male, a female and the remaining person was difficult to identify because they wore a black hooded sweater that concealed part of their face. The male that arrived was a heavyset man. His hair was straggly and looked greasy. I could see the lens of his glasses glisten as cars drove by with their bright headlights. The girl was shorter than everyone there. She wore pants, a sweater and a jacket with a scarf around her neck with her hair in a high ponytail. Her backpack hung off her right shoulder. The headlight of cars going by caused the buttons on her backpack to shine and showed the color of her bag, it looked yellow, but I wasn't sure. Although I was far, I made out something else on her backpack, it looked like a poppy that one would wear on Remembrance Day. With aching legs, we stayed crouched, trying to listen to what they were saying.

"Does anyone have any leads?" asked a voice that sounded a lot like Mr. Henry.

The rest of the individuals murmured, but we couldn't make out one thing that was being said. Finally, we gave up and went back inside.

Noreen was waiting for us in the spot we agreed on and we decided it was time to go home. I knew I witnessed something tonight that was not quite right. One thing's for sure: everyone standing in that alleyway had something to hide, and I intended to find out exactly what that was.

On the car ride home, we all sat in silence. I couldn't help but wonder what Mr. Henry was doing out there in the alley. Sophia dropped us off; I went straight to my room, peeled off my dress, kicked my heels off, showered and flat-lined onto my bed.

The sound of screams filled my ears. I could smell the smoke, so I covered my nose with the top part of my nightgown. I looked down at myself and I had on a white nightie that went down to my feet. My feet and hands were smaller. How is that possible?

Sweat poured from my head as the heat from the flames beat down on me. Again I saw people I recognized but this time was a bit different. I saw what looked like an older Mr. Henry screaming and running from the fire. His hair was more grey, and his face wrinkled. The anger that once fuelled this blaze started to die down as confusion consumed my every being. Why is Mr. Henry here? Before I had time to digest that question, a girl stood in front of me. She stood staring directly at me as if she was looking straight into my soul. Suddenly she turned around and started running, that is when I saw her yellow bag with the buttons. She ran straight into the arms of a man who wore all back with the hood from his sweater covering his head. He grabbed her and led her to safety away from the flames. As he put his arm around her shoulders, it looked like a symbol was tattooed on his hand and fore…

Breathing heavily, I woke up hot with perspiration. I got out of bed, went to the bathroom and washed my face with cool water. Why did I dream about Mr. Henry or any of those people, for that matter? Were they in my subconscious because I saw them the night before? It left me feeling unsettled and puzzled. I pushed those thoughts from my mind and forced myself back to sleep.

Chapter 3

The next morning, I woke up with a slight headache. Great… a hangover. I still couldn't get the events from my nightmare out of my thoughts. I rummaged through my nightstand drawer and brought out a bottle of Advil. I went to the kitchen with capsel in hand and got a bottle of water to it wash down. Once the medication started to set in, I took a hot shower.

With a towel tied around my body and a t-shirt around my wet hair, I received a text message from Sophia asking to meet for brunch. I messaged her back, agreeing to meet, and she sent me the address. I braided my hair, threw on my distressed jeans, a sweater, and my leather jacket, grabbed my sunglasses and was out the door.

When I got there, Sophia was already there. The smell of buttermilk pancakes and waffles gripped me. I could hear the sizzling of eggs in the frying pan and hash browns in the fryer. Children babbled while their parents spoke and laughed amongst each other. Every table was full at the restaurant; thankfully, Sophia was already sitting at a corner table waiting for me. As I approached, she stood to give me a one-armed hug.

"You look cute!" she said, looking at me up and down. "Love how you can go from formal to casual with such ease. Not many have that talent," she said matter-of-factly.

Talent? She can't be serious, I thought to myself.

"Uh, thanks? I guess…" I responded, unsure.

"You're welcome. You have to learn to accept compliments, Mya," Sophia said.

I couldn't roll my eyes hard enough as I laughed; she surely was growing on me. Of course, Sophia looked like she just stepped off the runway in New York Fashion Week. She wore a long sleeve navy blue jumpsuit that fit perfectly, her hair in a sleek high bun and doorknocker earrings. I sat down in the seat across from her and got comfortable.

"So last night was fun, right? Well, minus the sketchy stuff in that alleyway," Sophia said, lowering her voice.

A tall young male approached our table just as she finished speaking. He was probably around six feet tall with brown skin that looked smooth like the most expensive chocolate. His hair was cut in a crisp, low fade. The definition of his arms and pecks were visible through his work shirt, verifying that he was no stranger to the gym. Sophia stared at him like a cat in heat; I, on the other hand, tried to be a bit more discreet. His nametag said Levi with the title Assistant Manager.

"Have you guys had a chance to look at the menu?" Levi asked, showing his pearly white smile.

Sophia was too busy staring to hear his question, so I responded instead.

"Can I get the daily special? Pancakes, eggs but can I get turkey bacon instead of the regular one, please?" I smiled.

"I'll have what she's having," Sophia said, not even looking at the menu.

"Coming right up. Would you like a drink to start?" he asked.

Before having the chance to respond, the front door swung open, and a heavyset man with glasses and straggly greasy hair entered the restaurant. Instantly, the hairs on the back of my neck stood up, Sophia and I sat up straight in our chairs. We stared wide-eyed at each other; Sophia tilted her head towards the man as if to confirm that I was seeing what she was seeing. Neither of us noticed that Levi was watching our reaction the entire time. The man made his way around the restaurant, saying hello to all the staff. He passed Levi and patted him on the shoulder.

"How's the day going so far, Levi?" he asked.

"So far, so good, Chuck," Levi replied as his boss continued to walk. Levi then turned back to us. "I'll be right back with your food."

Sophia and I held our tongues until Levi was out of sight.

"Wasn't that the man we saw in the alleyway last night with Mr. Henry?" Sophia asked, barely able to contain herself. "This is crazy!"

"That was definitely him last night. I would recognize that greasy hair from anywhere," I said going over last night's happenings over again in my head.

"What do you think he was doing meeting Mr. Henry at almost two o'clock in the morning? They must have something going on, right?" Sophie said, looking at me for answers.

"Honestly, I have no idea. But low-key, I kind of want to find out," I said right as our food was brought to the table steaming hot by a smiling female waitress.

Sophia nodded in agreement. "Me too," she whispered.

We ate our food without stopping. I was starving, but if I were to be honest, I couldn't wait to get out of that restaurant. I looked up at Sophia as she stuffed her face with eggs and pancakes at the same time; I think, for once, we were on the same page. We finished our plates and waited for the bill. We paid for our meals in cash, and Levi came back with our receipts, mine had a handwritten note on the back.

We need to talk ASAP. Call me so we can meet #416-555-0101-Levi

I discreetly folded the receipt, put it in my back pocket, and smiled at him. Sophia and I thanked him for our food and left the restaurant. Before closing the door behind me, I looked back to see Levi looking at me with urgency in his eyes. I turned around and closed the door behind me. What could he possibly have to speak to me about? Sophia and I said our goodbyes and went our separate ways. I could tell she was deep in thought as she wasn't her normal, cheerful self.

The weekend flew by as always, and Monday came with a vengeance. Still exhausted from the weekend, I had to push myself to go to my eight o'clock newspaper Reporting class. I love writing, but taking this Journalism course has confirmed one thing for me: I do NOT want to be a newspaper reporter. Not that there's anything wrong with it, if that's your sort of thing that is. I enjoy writing pieces that take you into another world and forces you to see things in ways your mind couldn't think up yourself. So imagine my glee when our professor was off sick, and we were able to leave early. I went outside to the courtyard for some air and sat down at a picnic table, relaxing, enjoying the cool breeze and the warm sun. A group of three girls sat at the same table but on the opposite side from where I was. At first, I paid them no mind, as their conversation was regular gossip and girl chat, that is, until their conversation took a turn I didn't expect.

"Speaking of rumours... did you guys ever hear about that town that caught on fire years ago?" the first girl said, smacking her gum.

"Yea, I remember hearing a few people talk about it, but I didn't believe it for a second. If it were true, it would have been on the news, and for sure, the person would've been caught. It all sounds like a load of bullocks if you ask me," another girl chimed in with an English accent.

"It was said the whole town was on fire, and apparently, no one knows what started it. The suspect was never found either, but I heard everyone survived, but many were injured," the third girl added.

"Why are we still talking about this? The story is rubbish! The end." the British-sounding girl said, sounding annoyed.

Listening to the girls speak, I could feel panic and anxiety start to rise and sit in my throat. I flashed back to my nightmare with everyone running from the flames. I started to breathe rapidly, and my vision began to go hazy as I gripped the sides of the bench for support. My palms were drenched with sweat, and it became more difficult to hold on to the bench seat. I wish they would stop talking, I thought. Straightaway, the three girls stopped talking and sat in silence. The panicking started to cease, and my breathing eventually levelled out. I've never felt so grateful for people to stop talking.

I looked up to see Zohrah and her friend walking up ahead and I had to blink twice to ensure I was seeing correctly. Zohrah's friend had on a yellow backpack with buttons and a red Remembrance Day poppy. Once I felt back to my normal self, I wiped my palms along my jeans, got up and jogged over to them.

"Hey! Zohrah?" I called out of breath when I caught up.

"Hey, Mya. How's it going?" she asked.

"I just wanted to apologize for the way I acted the other day in the hallway. I was pretty rude," I said, looking at her friend from the corner of my eye.

"Thanks, I appreciate that."

I extend my hand to Zohrah's friend to introduce myself.

"I'm Mya. And you are?" I ask, extending my hand.

"Uhh, Karina", she replied, shaking my hand.

"I like the buttons on your backpack. It's not often you see a poppy... unless it's November," I pointed out.

"Yea, I feel like Remembrance Day should always be celebrated, not just in November... I mean, unless you don't think the people who risked their lives to serve during the war should be remembered," she said.

"You've made your point. It's just out of the norm, that's all," I cut her off before she could go on. "But man, I love the color of your knapsack… I mean, it's bright, but I like it," I say, obviously reaching for anything at this point.

Karina stares at me for a moment, unsure of how to respond.

"I'm not sure if there was a compliment in there somewhere," she responded, staring directly into my eyes.

"You seem defensive when all I said was…"

"It just kind of feels like you're fishing, that's all…" Karina said, cutting me off.

"Why would I be fishing? I don't even know you?" I asked, smiling.

I knew what I was doing… and so did she. I kept her gaze for a moment. Zohrah was staring at us in disbelief; I could sense her irritation with the tension.

"Wow… Z let me know when … she leaves," Karina glared at me, then marched off.

"Perfect, Zohrah. I need to speak to you privately anyway," I said, hoping this conversation goes well.

Without question, Karina stalked away, leaving us alone. Zohrah and I walked further into the courtyard amongst the trees.

"Sheesh… is she always like this?" I asked.

"Like what?"

"Defensive… over the top… pick one," I laugh. She doesn't. "How long have you guys been friends?"

"Long enough," she answered shortly.

This wasn't going to be easy.

"Would you say you know her well? Has she ever done anything that would make you question her loyalty?" I asked.

"Are you okay?"

"Excuse me?"

"Who do you think you are coming here and asking me all these questions about my best friend and you don't know either of us!" she scolded.

This was the first time in a long time I was speechless.

"I… well, I was just curious to know…"

"It's none of your business, Mya!" she spat. "Back off!"

The more Zohrah got upset, pebbles, pinecones, and everything around us began to rattle and shake against the surface under them. Zohrah looked around and slowly started to calm herself down and everything around us came to a halt. She inhaled, then exhaled and forced a smile.

"Sorry for the outburst. I just don't like being questioned by someone I don't know well," Zohrah explained.

"I understand, and I apologize for being so aggressive. I'll let you get back to Karina; see you around," I replied, feeling defeated.

Zohrah nodded and walked away, looking for her friend. I turned around and went in the opposite direction. Something was off about that conversation. I could almost feel her wrath projecting from her body; I'd never felt something so strong before. Even the ground below me was humming and tickling my feet. Maybe it was all in my imagination, that sort of thing can't be real… can it?

As I walked, I put my hand into my back pocket and felt a piece of paper; unfolding the paper, I realized it's the receipt with Levi's number on it. I remembered the urgency on his face as I left the restaurant that day. I had nothing to lose by calling him and listening to what he had to say. I pulled my phone out and started dialling his number.

Watching from a distance, I could see Zohrah getting irritated from that Mya girl speaking to her. Who does she think she is anyway? Questioning me like she knows something. I've always been discreet about my endeavours, so there's no possible way she knows anything about me or… What could she be saying that has Zohrah so frazzled? Wait… something on the ground is moving. Everything around them seems to be… vibrating against their surface. No! This can't be happening. I've known Zohrah for years, and I never would have thought for a second she was… one of US. For so long, I've been searching for someone else like me… someone else with abilities, and she was right under my nose the whole time. Why didn't she tell me! She shouldn't have had to do this by herself; she must have felt so alone. I must let the others know what I've discovered. Karina turned around and disappeared back behind a tree.

Chapter 4

Zohrah

Past

It was a very hot day. The sun beat down on me as I kicked the soccer ball back and forth with my five-year-old brother Jamal. The sound of playful screaming filled the air as the neighbourhood children were outside. A few boys had buckets of water to pour on their heads to cool down from the extreme heat. They tried to spray others to start a water fight. A group of girls sang songs and clapped along. The women laughed amongst themselves as they watched their children play happily. It was all around a great day.

In the evening our house was filled with my family that came to celebrate my tenth birthday. I loved it when everyone came to visit us; I could feel that I was surrounded by love. My younger cousins danced in the living room while my mother served everyone my favourite chocolate cake that she baked herself. When dessert was finished, and everyone was sitting around watching T.V, one of my uncles flipped through the channels to find something appropriate for the children to watch when he saw the news and stopped for moment.

On the television, people were running in the streets, yelling and causing chaos, while the news reporter stated that the Prime Minister of Lebanon was assassinated in a car bombing earlier that evening. In the background, I could hear the people chanting, others were fighting and being rebellious. My father turned the TV off and sent the children to my room to play. I sat still, trying to digest what my eyes just perceived. I suddenly felt uneasy, and I became worried that something terrible was going to happen to my family. My father kneeled down beside me on the carpet; he held my shoulder like he knew my thoughts. He pulled me into one of his famous big hugs that I love and whispered into my ear not to worry, and everything would be fine.

Nightfall came quickly. The rest of my family went home and Jamal and I were in bed asleep. I heard what sounded like our front door open but paid no attention to it as I drifted back to sleep. The abrupt, piercing sound of my mother's scream made me sit up in my bed at attention. I checked on Jamal, who was now stirring in his bed. I waited until I heard his stable, heavy breathing, and I crept out of our room and I shut the door behind me. Careful not to make a sound, I tiptoed down the hall to the living room. As I got closer, I heard what sounded like a struggle between my father and someone else. I crouched down and crawled on the floor and hid behind the couch so I could get a better look. I peeked from behind the couch, there were three men, all armed with weapons. I stared at the men's faces to see if I recognized them, but I did not. One man had my father face down on the ground with a rifle pointed at his head. The second man had a handgun pointed at my mother with one hand while he fought with her to take off her clothes with his free hand. The third man was keeping watch by the door. It took everything in me not to scream. I covered my mouth with both hands and tried to calm down and think of a plan.

"Take off your clothes," the man said to my mother.

My mother looked at him and spat in his face. He slapped her across her face so hard it left her cheek bruised and swollen. My father started to fight on the ground as the other gunman pushed the rifle harder onto my father's head, warning him to stop.

"Hurry up and finish with her so I can have my turn," said the man by the door.

"Please!" my mother pleaded. "You don't have to do this. We'll do anything you want."

"The only thing I want you to do is shut your mouth and do as you're told," the man said while rubbing his face in the nape of her neck. He licked the sweat off her face as my mother cringed with disgust, and tears streamed down her face. My father continued to fight on the ground and yelling in frustration, wanting to save his wife.

Suddenly, a bedroom door opened from the hallway, and Jamal came running out to the living room. Realizing what was happening, I tried to pull him aside as he ran past the couch I hid behind, but I missed him. I whispered his name, trying to get his attention, but it was too late. All the men turned to see Jamal; they looked almost shocked like they didn't realize there were children living here. My mother screamed and pleaded with the men to let him go.

"Go back in your room son, please!" my father smiled, trying to make it seem like everything was ok.

The third man by the door pulls out his gun from the holster around his waist, points it at Jamal and pulls the trigger. Jamal flew back from the impact of the bullet as it connected to his chest. Screams from my mother and father rang throughout the house. Jamal lay on the floor beside the couch where I hid. He looked directly at me and blinked once as blood started to flow from his mouth. Trembling, I reached for him, touching his face as the life left his eyes.

The feeling of rage rushed over me as I sat there looking at my baby brother on the ground. I opened my mouth and screamed as loud as I could. I stood up and started walking from behind the couch. The gunmen looked at me as they yelled at each other about what they should do next. Anger continued to take over my body; it bubbled up and overflowed. With my hands clenched into fists at my side, I kept screaming. Tired of my shrieking and not wanting any more unnecessary attention, the third gunman grabbed his weapon and pointed it at me. Just then, everything in the house started to vibrate against their surface. I looked around but was too blinded by anger to care what was happening. The gunmen looked around, wondering what that sound was. Slowly, knives and other utensils from the kitchen started to ascend. The vase on the windowsill, toys on the ground and the plates from the dinning room table started to levitate into the air and then spin around everyone violently as they all stood still. I took another breath and continued to scream as I walked towards the gunmen, staring directly into their eyes.

The third gunman moved his index finger onto the trigger, and right before he squeezed, his gun lifted into the air and whipped around the room with the other objects. The man who shot Jamal tried to lunge at me when a butcher knife from the kitchen stabbed him in the back, ripping through his abdomen. Blood sprayed from the wound, and my mother screamed in horror. The knife tore through his thoracic cavity, and his lifeless body dropped to the floor as a pool of blood started to pour from beneath him. The other two intruders looked at their dead friend nervously. The second gunman finally let go of my mother and attempted to run towards the door. The rifle stopped circling the room, aimed at his groin and fired. He dropped to his knees, shrieking in agony, realizing too late that the gun was now levelled with his forehead. He tried to move out of its way but wasn't fast enough; the bullet left the muzzle, leaving his brain matter splattered across the carpet.

The last man looks from one friend to the other, who lay dead on the floor. He looked up at my parents, realizing there was no hope left for him. He grabbed the handgun from the air, as it was about to move past him, put the muzzle in his mouth and pulled the trigger. In that moment everything that was in the air fell to the ground. Completely drained, I collapsed to the floor and sobbed uncontrollably. My parents rushed to my side, and we all cried together as we mourned Jamal.

"You saved us, Zohrah," my father cried while brushing strands of hair away from my face.

I looked up at my parents and I could see in their eyes they were overcome with emotions from what they witnessed tonight. I myself was unsure about what happened. One minute, I was scared, and the next, I felt rage and invincible.

"You're different. And that's okay we love you all the same," my mother said. "But Zohrah, you must promise never to speak of this to anyone. What happened hear tonight must never be repeated… understood?" She enforced while holding my cheeks in her hands and staring at me in my eyes.

I nodded in agreeance, although I still felt confused about what just happened. I looked back at my brother's lifeless body on the floor and continued to cry until I had nothing left in me.

Present

I sat on a bench in the school courtyard, pushing that memory from my mind. That was the last time I was with my family back in Lebanon. I often feel homesick but that memory puts everything back in perspective. After realizing I was different, my parents sent me to live here in Canada with my aunt and cousins. They felt I would be safer here. I haven't been back since, but I always made sure I kept the promise I made to my mother. Nobody must know of my ability.

I wiped away a tear before it could roll down my cheek, stood up and continued to look for Karina. I was still angry with Mya for trying to pry and questioning my friend's loyalty to me. There was a moment I almost lost control, something like that must never happen again. Although I hated being questioned about Karina, a part of me feels… actually, I know Karina has done some questionable things. But what would make Mya question Karina when she doesn't know her?

I walked up and down the courtyard, searching for Karina, Where could she have gone? I could hear the footsteps of rushing students heading back inside to get to class. I checked my watch, three minutes until my next class, so I turned and walked back to the school. I'll probably see Karina after class. I took one last scan across the yard, still no Karina, so I left.

Class went by quickly; I couldn't get my brother and parents out of my thoughts. I leave the classroom, still keeping an eye out for Karina; it's a bit weird that she would disappear like that. We usually travel home together every day. I decided to walk around for a bit to see if I'd bump into her before going home. I walked down the hall, and as I was about to turn a corner, I noticed Karina down the corridor. I duck back behind the wall so she doesn't see me and poke my head out, still remaining undetected. Karina is standing in the hallway, speaking with two other people. One was a teacher from this school, I don't have his class. Thinking back I believe I've seen Mya leaving his classroom. The second person was also a male; I'd never seen him before. He wore black cargo pants, a black long-sleeve shirt and a baseball cap that had a Red Sox symbol on the front. They spoke to each other as if trying to be inconspicuous but failed tremendously.

As I stood there for a moment just watching, I saw further down the hall, Mya was facing a bulletin board that had all the upcoming school activities listed, however, I noticed Mya kept glancing upward. I followed her stare and saw that she was using the convex mirror to spy on the conversation taking place between Karina, the Mr. Henry and the mystery man behind her. Her friend was talking, oblivious to what was going on behind them. Unexpectedly, Mya turns and looks in my direction and catches me staring at her. We pause for a moment; then she turns to her friend, and they both leave.

Just as I started to feel ridiculous for snooping on my best friend, Karina turned around and reached for the doorknob leading to a classroom behind them and went in. Mr. Henry went in next, and the third male stood for a moment in the hallway, looking left and right. I ducked back behind the wall to make sure I wasn't seen. When I peeked again, I caught a glimpse of the door closing. I wish I knew what was going on behind that door; I wanted to believe it was nothing, but I knew I would by lying to myself. I'll ask her about it tomorrow when I see her hopefully, everything will get cleared up then.

The next day I was eager to meet with Karina to get to the bottom of what I saw the day before. I couldn't erase the scenario from my mind. I texted her a few times last night but got no response, which again, I found odd. While walking to school, I noticed Karina's bright backpack up ahead, so I picked up my pace to catch up.

"Karina!" I yelled while jogging behind her. "Wait up!"

She slowed down for me to catch up. I paused for a moment to take a breather.

"What happened to you yesterday? I was looking for you everywhere," I asked, hoping she would tell me the truth.

"Huh… Oh, yesterday… I went home," she said timidly. "Didn't I tell you I was leaving?"

"Uh, no! I messaged you and everything last night. You had me worried for a minute there. So after you spoke with Mya yesterday you went home?" I asked, giving one last chance to come clean.

"Yes! What's with the third degree?" Karina asked, sounding slightly irritated.

"Nothing. Just wanted to make sure," I said, remembering the hallway yesterday.

I walked the rest of the way to school in silence. Off and on I heard Karina rambling about different things, but I wasn't listening. I was too focused on wondering why my so-called best friend was lying to my face. Could Mya have been right about her all along? Karina is the first friend I've had since living in Canada. I can't imagine being betrayed by her.

Five years ago

The first day of high school I was a nervous wreck. I left Lebanon five years prior and I managed to keep my distance from my school peers and my family here in Canada in fear of repeating what happened years ago. I was an official loner, and I preferred it that way.

I walked down the halls of Trinity Academy with my backpack on my back. I pulled out my schedule to find my homeroom. I walked into the class and sat down quietly, waiting for the teacher to introduce himself. I felt someone tap my shoulder from behind me, so I turned to see who it was.

"Don't you hate first days? Everyone sits quietly, looking at each other; no one wants to break the ice. I hate the first days. I prefer to jump right in head first," the girl said, looking at me as if waiting for a response.

"Uh, yea. Agreed," I said, then turning back to face the front.

"I'm Karina, by the way. What's your name?" she asked.

"Zohrah."

"Pretty. Where are you from? I've never seen you here before. Did you come from another school?"

"I'm from Lebanon," I said, not interested in continuing this conversation.

"Cool! Did you just move here?"

"No, I've been here for a few years."

Just then, the teacher saved me and started talking, or so I thought.

"Hey!" Karina whispered. "Let's hang out at lunch. You down?"

I thought for a moment, *What do I have to lose?*

"Sure, why not," I whispered back.

"Girls... can this conversation wait until after class?" The teacher asked, but we both knew it wasn't a question but a warning.

From that day forward, we've been inseparable.

Present

"Zohrah! Hey! I don't even know how we've been friends for this long. You never listen to me," Karina said, ripping me from my memories.

"Sorry. My mind is elsewhere," I said as I looked up to realize we arrived at our destination.

"Well as I was saying... we should go out to lunch tomorrow. There's this new place I heard about that I want to try. You down?"

"Always."

Walking away from Karina, I felt a sudden rush of restlessness that I couldn't shake; something was off. I turned to look back in her direction, and she was still looking at me, walk away. I can't believe she would lie to my face and do it with such ease. It's obvious this isn't her first rodeo either, how many times has she lied, and I was too blind to see it. Did Mya have a point in what she was saying? There must have been something she saw why she was questioning Karina in the first place. Finally I waved bye to Karina and kept moving.

The next day rolled around, and my stomach growled angrily as lunch hour drew near. I left my class and went outside to wait for Karina to go eat. The sun was shining, but the air was still crisp and chilly. As she arrived, something seemed different. She seemed nervous or anxious; I couldn't put my finger on it. Also,

I was way too hungry to care. Karina smiled as she approached me.

"Ready?" she asked, swinging her backpack to one shoulder.

"Ready as I'll ever be. Where are we headed?" I asked curiously.

"It's this new burrito place. It's about a ten-minute walk from here."

"Alright, lets go," I said while letting her lead the way.

Neither of us spoke for a while. My mind was swarming with questions, but the biggest of all was how could I trust Karina knowing what I know? I can't be friends with someone that I can't trust. With everything I've been through in my past, this is the last thing I needed. Granted, Karina knows nothing about my family or my secret, but that is for her protection. Then Karina stopped and turned to walk down an alleyway, I stopped, unsure whether to follow.

"It's right down this way," she said, stopping and turning around as she realized I wasn't walking beside her anymore. "What's wrong?"

"I'm not sure. I was just wondering why this way?" I questioned.

"Uh, it's a short cut duh! What is with you today? What, you don't trust me or something?"

I stood and examined the path. My stomach was in knots; I knew something wasn't right. At the same time, we were alone, so what could Karina possibly do to me that I couldn't handle on my own? After a moment, I started walking to meet up with her in the alley. I looked up at the colourful abstract graffiti that filled the walls. Suddenly, I heard something drop behind us, I turned quickly but saw nothing.

"Did you hear that?" I asked, trying to keep my heart from racing.

"Hear what? Since when are you so jumpy? We're in an alley, Zohrah. It could be anything. It could have been garbage falling from that dumpster down there. Now come ooonn, I'm starving!" she said, pulling my arm to keep walking.

I turned and kept moving. We were half way down the alleyway when I noticed Karina was very fidgety, and she kept looking back like she was expecting someone or something.

"Everything okay?" I asked distrustfully.

"Yea... well no… I mean, ok, so I have a confession to make," Karina said as she stopped walking and faced me.

"I'm listening," I said as I sighed with relief. Finally, she was going to tell me the truth! I was worried and doubting for no reason at all.

"I'm not sure how to say this, so I'll just come out and say it. I know … that you're different," she said, staring, waiting for my reaction.

"Wha... what are you talking about?" I asked, taking a step back.

"I know about your ability. And you don't have to worry, Zohrah; you don't have to live a lie anymore. We can help you."

I was beyond stunned. For a moment, I had to remind myself to breathe. How could she have known? All I know now is I need to get away from her as soon as possible. I could hear my mother's voice reminding me to never let anyone know about my ability. Deny, deny, deny!

"I have no clue what you're talking about, but I must say your imagination is outstanding. I think I better go," I said, trying to step aside to get past her.

"I'm sorry, Zohrah, we can't let you leave," she said, stepping in front of me. "But like I said, we can help you if you let us. I promise nothing will happen to you," she said, reaching to touch my shoulder.

"Wait… who's we?" I asked, I pulled way from her grasp, taking another step back, I felt a body bump me from behind.

Startled, I turned quickly to see the two men I saw Karina speaking with in the hallway yesterday, the teacher from school and the man in all black. Both of them watched at me with ravenous eyes with dilated pupils. I was surrounded and had no place to run.

"It will be painlessZohrah, trust me," Karina said squeezing my shoulder from behind.

"Trust *YOU?*" I spat. "How dare you deceive me in such a tremendous way. I *TRUSTED* you. You were my best friend... my *ONLY* friend, and this is how you repay me? You just throw me to the wolves?"

The sound of clapping drew my attention away from Karina; I turned to the man wearing all black, laughing hysterically.

"Bravo, ladies, bravo indeed. That was touching... it really was. But see, the thing is Karina dear, how do I put this lightly... well, we lied," he said as though it was second nature.

I examined him as much as I could. He wore black pants and a black hooded sweater, similar to what he had worn yesterday, except today no baseball hat. Instead, he had his hood covering his head. As he spoke, he pushed his sleeves up his forearm, revealing his tattoo of a symbol on his hand leading up his forearm. His face was clean-cut and well-groomed. He looked like he could be a real charmer if he wanted. His smile of satisfaction spread across his mouth. I looked back at Karina as she argued with one of the men, her face oozed with fear and anger for being misled. Get in line.

"You've got to be kidding me!" Karina yelled. "What do you mean you lied? Wh…why would you lie? You said that there's another way now! You said you found a way that was painless and easy!"

"Yes, I did say that, didn't I," he smirked. "Well, Ms. Karina, I wish I had better news for you. You'll make new friends. There's more fish in the sea… I've heard people use that line before, hopefully, it helps."

While they had their exchange of words, I took this opportunity to run past Karina, who leapt out the way to let me go. I scream with everything in me, hoping someone will come to my rescue.

"ZOHRAH RUN!" Karina bellowed as I sprinted to the end of the alley.

Just as I reached the sidewalk, two arms grabbed me from behind and dragged me back into the darkness. I stomped on his foot, and he shrieked with pain and fury. He hauled me back and stood me in front of the man wearing black.

"You're a little firecracker, aren't you," he said as he tilted his head to the left and lifted his hands to touch my face. "Any last words?" he whispered, coming closer.

"Malachi, don't do this. There has to be another way!" Karina pleaded as Mr. Henry held her still.

I looked around, and I knew this was it for me. I had nothing left in me and nothing left to fight for. My parents are distant with me, and my brother is dead when I could have saved him. Right now giving in seemed like my best option, my only option. Malachi lifted me by my neck into the air with one arm. My vision started to blur because of the lack of oxygen going through my windpipe. I kicked, trying to get down, but there was no use, he was stronger than me. I could hear Karina crying and yelling in the background and Mr. Henry ordering her to shut up or she'll be next. Malachi stared at me intently and both his eyes went entirely black. His face began to contort as his mouth opened wider than humanly possible. He breathed in, and that was when the excruciating pain took over my body. I yelled in agony. My physique felt like it was slowly being split apart from head to toe. I couldn't think or focus on anything but the pain. I could feel myself shrinking as my garments hung off my skin, they weren't snug like it was moments prior. The skin on my hands and face started to wrinkle and sag. I knew exactly what was taking place, and I could feel the life being ripped out of me. This is what it must feel like to die.

Suddenly I heard a 'thud' as bodies dropped behind me, which distracted Malachi for a moment. Then abruptly, he released his grip, allowing me to fall the ground as he was swept high into the air and thrown into a graffiti-filled wall, knocking him unconscious. In a daze, I heard two sets of footsteps running towards me, but I was too weak to lift my head. I saw their shadow figures kneeling over me for a moment right before it went dark.

56

Chapter 5

"Hello?"

"Hi, is this Levi? This is Mya, the girl from the restaurant," I said, praying he remembered me and this wasn't just some ploy to get me to call him.

"Hey. Yea, I remember you. I can't talk right now; I just started my shift at work. Can I message you tomorrow if that's ok with you?"

"Yea, that's fine. This is my cell, so you can text me at this number," I say, trying not to sound too disappointed.

We both hang up. I stood in the courtyard, wondering where to go next. I checked my schedule to see what my next class was and then checked the time. Three minutes to get to my Magazine writing class on time… I want to get there quickly as it is one of my favourite classes (being top of that class doesn't hurt either). I followed the crowd and rushed back into the school; I gazed over to see Zohrah still looking around. She still hasn't found Karina? I pushed thoughts of our awkward conversation to the back of my head and stepped through the school doors, letting them swing shut behind me.

Feeling winded from running, I made it to class right before the teacher closed the door. I quickly sit down and pull my books out of my bag. I get comfortable trying to mentally prepare.

I'm back in the hallway at school. That was fast! I turned to see Sophia speaking beside me about… something; I couldn't make out what she was saying. I looked behind me, and Karina was standing with two men, one being Mr. Henry, and the third male was someone I hadn't seen here before. Their conversation seemed to be intense. I stared into their faces, realizing none of them could see me. The unidentified man rolled his sleeves, revealing his left arm, and a tattoo of a symbol caught my eye.

Snapping out of my vision, I was back in class, and the teacher was talking. I looked around the room nervously, hoping there wouldn't be another repeat of Mr. Henry's class. Thankfully, nobody suspected a thing, so I caught up on notes from the person sitting next to me.

Class ended and I was trying to piece my last vision together in my head. Sophia ran up to me as I walked. I couldn't tell you what she was talking about because it's hard to focus after what just happened. Sophia stopped me in front of the school bulletin board.

"I need a job," Sophia stated as she looked through the different available positions posted. "Help me look, Mya!"

I scan the board, pointing out a few that might be of interest to her. Of course, she declines all of them. Then, I hear two familiar voices behind me. Mr. Henry and a female who sounds a lot like Karina. I couldn't make out exactly what they were saying; I only heard bits and pieces. I wanted to turn around, but I knew that wouldn't be a good idea. I stood there thinking of another way to see behind me when I noticed a convex mirror close to the ceiling. I slowly shifted my head slightly but mainly used my eyes to look up. I saw that it was definitely Karina speaking to Mr. Henry, but there was a third person. A male from what I could tell, wearing mainly black and the vision I had moments ago came flooding back. The man in black rolled his sleeve up, displaying what looked like a symbol on his arm. Was it the same from my vision? It's too hard to tell... I fought the urge to turn around and kept my head straight ahead. The sound of Sophia's voice suddenly caught my attention.

"What's she doing over there?" she whispered.

Looking to my right, I see Zohrah peeking from behind a wall, looking at me. We caught eyes, and for that moment, I knew she had seen something she didn't like. Something she knew wasn't right, but she couldn't figure it out either. After all, she wouldn't be hiding behind a wall spying on her "bestie" if my suspicions about her weren't true.

"Ugh, let's go," Sophia says, pulling my arm. "There's nothing here that interests me. I'll check again next week."

Hesitantly, I agree, and we leave.

My phone vibrated, it was a text from Levi asking to meet for lunch tomorrow. A smile tugged at the corner of my lips as I sent a quick reply agreeing to his request.

"What are you smiling about?" Sophie asked, trying to peek at my text.

"Nothing, really. Just Levi asking to meet for lunch tomorrow… to talk," I said, putting my phone in my back pocket.

"Levi..Levi? Wait you mean the sexy guy from brunch the other day? When did this happen? When did he even get your number?" Sophia demanded.

"That's a long story," I answer, not wanting to explain everything. "But he said he has something to talk to me about, so I'm going to hear him out over lunch tomorrow."

"Where are you going? Want me to come? What if he's some kind of creeper," Sophia looked at me with concerned eyes.

"At this new Mexican place around the corner from here. And I appreciate the offer, but I really think I can take care of myself," I said, checking the time. "I have to head home. I'll see you tomorrow, alright?"

"Fine. We'll talk later," Sophia said, not liking it one bit.

That night, I focused on putting the pieces of my vision together. What could Karina, Mr. Henry and the anonymous man have in common? They are obviously hiding something but it seems like they are either getting sloppy or they want to get caught. And then there's Levi; what could he have to speak to me about, considering he doesn't know me. I have no choice but to wait and see what he wants, there's no way I'm figuring out anything tonight. I closed my eyes to get some rest.

Smoke filled my lungs as I coughed and fanned the fumes from my face. I could feel the heat from the blaze beating down on me as everyone in the town screamed and ran for their lives. The anger I felt for these people was overwhelming. They judged me. The look in their eyes spoke volumes; how could they allow this sort of thing to happen? The more I thought, the more the flames grew and multiplied. Karina stood looking at me for a moment, then ran into the arms of the man in all black. From the corner of my eye, I saw a female with fire on her head, when I looked closer, I noticed it was Noreen, and her hair danced around her face as she ran. Suddenly, a calming voice came from behind me.

"It's ok, sweetie. You don't have to do this. Not everyone will understand, but this is not the answer, sweetheart."

I looked over to see a young woman kneeling beside me, looking at me with love in her eyes. Straightaway, I felt safe. Who is she?

"Just let go of this anger, Mya and come with me. I will keep you safe. I love you, Mya; you can trust me," she said, looking into my eyes.

The woman had short black coils in her hair and the most amazing piercing brown eyes I've ever seen. Something about her looked familiar… if felt as if I was looking into a mirror of the future. She looked like me but different. She smiled and I felt within my heart I could trust her. I took her hand and…

I woke up in a jolt to Noreen standing in my bedroom doorway looking at me.

"Was I loud? Sorry, Nor," I said, rubbing my eyes.

"It wasn't that. You said my name this time," she replied as she walked into my bedroom.

"Damn! I did? To be honest Nor, I don't remember much after I wake up. It's kind of a blur," I lied. I knew I couldn't tell Noreen what I saw in my nightmare before I figured out what it all meant.

"I don't believe you," she said, now coming closer and sitting on my bed. "Talk to me; you can trust me."

"Well, you don't have to believe me… it's the truth whether you like it or not," I lied, yet still felt defensive. "But maybe another time you can help me depict my dream… help jog my memory… but right now I'm too tired," I fixed my pillow, wishing she'd take the hint and leave me alone.

Immediately, Noreen was on her feet and walking to the door. Her reaction took me by surprise. I expected her to put up more of a fight, but I wasn't going to complain.

"Have a good night, Mya. If you need to talk, you know where I'll be," she said, sounding hurt I wouldn't tell her the truth, and then she closed my door.

Once the coast was clear, I sat up in my bed and pulled open my nightstand drawer revealing a small notebook and pen. I thought it would be a good idea to start taking notes whenever these dreams occurred. These nightmares are nothing like I've experienced before. In the past, when I've had a bad dream, once I wake up, its difficult to recall anything. However, these nightmares… no matter what, I always managed to remember every single detail. I jot down the names of the people I saw tonight, and everyone so far are people I've been suspicious of, but not Noreen. She's my good friend so why was she there? And who was the mystery woman speaking to me… calming me down? It's strange that I felt like I knew her but I'm more than positive I've never seen her before. If my subconscious is trying to tell me something, it's doing a very poor job. I throw my notes and pen back into the drawer and lay back down.

The next day, I was anxious and excited about meeting with Levi. I couldn't help but wonder what he had to tell me. The weather was getting colder by the day so I wore my thick leggings, a long sweater, ankle boots and a warm jacket. I was at the restaurant first and I waited while drinking my lemon water. I sat by the window taking in the scenery. The place buzzed with families and friends chowing down on burrito bowls, tacos and quesadillas. The smell of different spices filled the air and made my mouth water. The front door opened, and Levi walked in, looking just as handsome as I remembered. He scanned the room and smiled when his eyes met mine; as he walked towards me, I noticed his dark denim jeans, a roots sweater, a thick jacket and a fresh pair of kicks. He pulled out his chair and, sat across from me and smiled. I had to stop myself from blushing and remind myself why we were here.

"What's your name again?" he said extending his hand out.

"Mya," I said, reaching to shake his hand. "And you're Levi," *Girl, DUH!* I thought to myself.

"Yep! Have you been here before?" he asked.

"No, but I've heard about it. Supposed to be really good," I answered, eyeing the menu, not daring to look at him.

Focus, Mya, I thought to myself.

We placed our orders, and while we waited for the food, Levi began to tell me why we were there.

"I know it's weird that I asked to meet you, but I have to go backwards to explain why you're here," he said as the waiter rested our food in front of us.

"Okay."

"The day you and your friend came for breakfast, earlier that day, I over heard my boss, Chuck Parnell is his name, speaking on the phone in his office. He didn't know I was listening, and I didn't hear everything. Just overheard the name Malachi," he said.

"For real? That's it?" I asked, waiting for him to get to the point.

"Let me finish," he said. "He kept saying he's keeping a close eye on things and something about knowing there's more out there and needing more power because he's getting weaker," he said in between chews.

"Power? What does he mean by that?" I asked, confused.

"That's not the worst part," Levi said, looking at me with wide eyes. I leaned in to hear better.

"What really had me was I heard him say, find them, strip them and get rid of them," Levi said as we sat there looking at each other dumbfounded.

I didn't know if I should believe him because, let's face it, we just met a few days ago. I sat looking at him, not totally convinced.

"Strip them can mean any… well, almost anything."

"True, but it's the 'get rid of them' part that has me thinking," he replied.

And he was right.

"So what happens now? We have no idea who he's talking about killing or what any of it means," I said to Levi while glancing out the window across the street.

Something caught my eye and I stopped instantaneously to make sure I saw correctly. I noticed a bright coloured backpack covered with buttons, and I knew exactly who that was. From the looks of it, she was conversing with someone in the alleyway. Her hand gestures insinuated she was trying to reason with them or get her point across. Sensing something was wrong, Levi followed my gaze.

"You know them?" he asked.

"Something like that," I replied, turning my attention back to him. "I lost my train of thought, where were we?"

At that moment, we heard a scream, and we both turned to see Zohrah running out of the alleyway. Two hands came from behind, covered her mouth and dragged her back into the dark path. Without saying a word, Levi and I ran out of the restaurant to help her. We ran across the street, and I was headed straight for the alley when Levi pulled me by my waist against the side of the building.

"What are you doing? She needs our help!" I spat angrily.

"Shhhhh… yes, but you can't just barge in there. You have to see what you're up against. Think about it, Mya!" he said with urgency.

We both peeked from behind the wall to see what was happening. Zohrah was yelling at Karina for betraying her. Mr. Henry was there standing beside the man I saw at school yesterday, which happens to be the same man from my vision.

"Those two girls go to my school. One of the men is my teacher, and the other guy in all black, I have an idea who he is, but I've seen him before," I whispered to Levi.

We could only hear the murmur of the man in black speaking; his demeanour seemed to have changed. He looked like a leader; he walked around with his head high and a cocky grin on his face as if he believed he was untouchable. I looked at Levi, wondering what we should do next, but he was looking down at his hands. I looked at his hands, too, and my eyes widened in disbelief. His hands looked like he was holding a bubble of some type of electric power source. It was transparent yet looked tangible. I looked at his face, and he looked just as confused as I felt.

"Wh… what is that?" I questioned, backing away from him.

"Right now, we need to focus on helping your friend," he said, moving his fingers slightly and nudging me behind him.

We peeked from behind the wall to see what was going on. Zohrah was being held up in the air while she kicked her feet vigorously, trying to get down as the man in black held her up with one arm. Karina was screaming for him to stop but was being held back by Mr. Henry.

"Malachi, stop this!" Karina yelled.

I felt a sea of goosebumps cover my skin and I noticed Levi's body tensed up when we heard the name Malachi mentioned. Then, the sound of ripping and an agonizing scream flooded my ears. Looking again, I noticed that Zohrah's hair was starting to turn a light grey color, her clothes began to sag, and her face wrinkled. Malachi stretched his mouth open wider than anything I'd ever seen before as he inhaled what seemed to be Zohrah's soul. My stomach turned from the gruesome sight and sounds, yet I couldn't turn away. I've never seen anything like this take place before. All of a sudden, Karina and Mr. Henry drop to the ground, which distracted Malachi. Once he loosened his grip on Zohrah, he flew to a nearby wall and was knocked unconscious. I turned to Levi wondering how Karina and those men were magically thrown into the air, but Levi was standing with his hands extended out in front of him in Malachi's direction. I stared at him, speechless.

"Wh...how?" were the only words I was able to say.

"Well... uh. There's a lot about me that...uh... I can't really explain right now... right now, you have to just trust me," Levi replied.

"Yea... right," I say, staring at him, unsure how to respond. "We need to get her out of here," I say, directing the conversation back to the task at hand.

We ran up to Zohrah to see if she was okay. From the looks of it, she would be lucky to still be alive.

Chapter 6

Levi

2 Days Prior

The piercing sounds of my mother yelling were deafening as I lay in my bed. I never understood why she continued to stay when this was a recurring dispute. Dishes crashed to the floor in the kitchen as I heard my mother and father wrestling with each other. I place one earphone in my ear to drown out my mom's crying and pleading for him to stop as my dad shouted for her to pick up what she dropped. Like clockwork the sound that came next always made my stomach clench with fury, the sound of his hand connecting to her skin echoed throughout our apartment. Closing my eyes, I recall the painful memory of when I tried to step in and help my mom but instead got ridiculed as she took her anger out on me.

"Get out, Levi!" she bellowed.

"But mom, how can yo…"

"Don't question me, boy! Stay out of grown folk business," she spat as she pushed me out the room.

My dad staggered around and told me to leave with his slurred speech. After that, I never tried to help her again, but I couldn't sit and listen to her get pulverised and do nothing. I grabbed my jogging pants, threw on my hoodie and jacket, snatched my phone and left.

I decided to take a walk to calm my nerves. The crisp night air was refreshing and soothing. As I walked down the street, I relished in the silence, the only sounds were from cars as they drove by. I take a walk around the block to avoid going home. As I turn a corner, I bump into a pretty girl with vibrant red hair. As my arm brushed her shoulder, I felt electricity pulsate throughout my body. It was something I'd never felt before.

"My bad," I said.

"It's alright," she replied and kept walking.

I continue to walk, and I can feel the energy surging through every inch of my body. I looked down at my hands, wondering what was happening to me. Just then, a group of young teenagers surrounded me, and I knew exactly what they wanted. Tonight, I was not in the mood to take part in these kid's silly shenanigans.

"Hey, I like your phone… let me see it real quick?" one of the boys said, reaching for it.

"Listen, this isn't what you want to do right now… any of you. Just go home, and we can forget this ever happened," I say, hoping they'll take the easy way out.

They laughed and stepped closer, challenging me.

"No, you listen. Give us your phone, and then YOU go home and forget this happened," the ringleader said, obviously wanting to show the others whose boss.

The boy stepped towards me, reaching for my arm to grab my phone. Quickly, I twisted his arm behind his back, placing my forearm around his neck in a chokehold.

"Listen, I'm giving you one last chance. Walk away," I said, slowly releasing my grip.

The young male staggered away, holding his neck angrily. He glared at me, and I stood my ground, hoping he would back down so we could move on. Suddenly, he leapt at me, swinging his fists. Not wanting to cause more of a scene, I hold my hands in front of me, warning him to stop. As my anger builds, I feel energy surge through my body. The boy lifts into the air and lands, sliding on his back on the sidewalk. With another flick of my wrist he slams into the side of a building. The male yelled out in agony, he stood up and ran with his friends trailing behind. I looked down at my still-tingling fingers, confused as to what had just taken place. I stood watching the scared boys scatter away from me, and some glanced back quickly as they ran to ensure they weren't being followed.

"Hey, are you okay?" a female voice asked from behind me.

I turned to see the same red-haired girl I bumped into not too long ago.

"Yea, I'm aight. Those kids just needed their asses kicked, that's all," I answered, hoping she didn't see everything.

"Understood. Well, I just wanted to make sure you were alright," she said, examining me. "See you around."

She started to walk away.

"What's your name?" I called out to her.

"Wouldn't you like to know?" she smiled and kept her stride.

I watched her for a moment as she left and then I turned head home.

The next day, I got up early for work, there was a dinner party happening at work tonight, and I needed to make sure everything ran smoothly. When I got there, my boss's car was already in the parking lot, yet when I walked in, all the lights were still off. I called out to him, but he didn't reply… *Maybe he just left his car here overnight,* I thought to myself. I walked to the back where Mr. Chuck Purnell's office was, and the closer I got I could hear his voice speaking to someone behind his office door. I lingered outside his door, waiting for his conversation to end, but the more I overheard, the more I couldn't help but eavesdrop.

"No leads yet… I'm keeping a close eye on… I need more power, I'm getting weaker by the day, and… I know there are more of them out… yes… find them, strip them and dispose of them… Got it."

I heard when Chuck put the phone down so I jogged down the hall and walked back towards his office to make it look like I was now arriving. Chuck opens his office door and spots me.

"Hey Levi, you're here early."

"Yea, I just got here. I wanted to get organized for the party tonight."

"Oh right, I forgot about that. Well, I won't hold you up from getting to work then. I'll be out for a few hours, but I'll be back before the lunchtime crowd. I'll see you later," he says, patting me on my shoulder.

Immediately, I feel a spark shoot through my body, very similar to the feeling I felt last night when I bumped into that red head girl.

"Alright, see you later then," I replied.

Levi is a great hard worker but I can only hope he didn't hear anything I just said while I was on the phone. There was something in his eyes that seemed like he knew something, but… ahh, it's probably my imagination. He was more than halfway down the hall when I opened my office door… there's no way he could have heard anything. He's a good kid… I'm just being paranoid. Sneaking around can be exhausting sometimes but I never used to such a duplicitous man. But for as long as I remember, I've always gone unnoticed and was overlooked my whole life became… well, let's just say I hated it. At home, my brother always got attention… he was slim… had thick hair… always got the girl, and my parents adored him. Me on the other hand… all I ever heard was, "Why can't you be like your brother Chuck?" I tried my best to ignore it, but I craved the feeling of power… of respect, and to be loved. I gave up on love years ago when I realized no woman would ever settle for a man like myself. I knew I had to build a name for myself, so I worked hard and became my own boss. I knew by doing that, I would finally get the respect I deserved by my family and peers. My employees have no choice but to listen, whether they agree with me or not.

When I met Malachi and the family of Syphoners, I was more than thrilled. When I was asked if I would join their syndicate… I didn't even have to think twice. This was exactly what I needed to feel powerful. And what we stand for may not be the norm… but in life, I learned early on it's every man for himself. And that is how I've gotten to where I am today. Since I've become a syphoner, I've been happier than ever. I have the respect I've always felt deserved… granted I've been shunned by my family, but let's face it… they barely cared for me anyway. I think this made it easier for them to do what they've always wanted to do… which is pretend I didn't exist. My mother "begged" me to join her and my father and become a Pacifist, but I declined. My brother joined the Agros and mentioned I should join him but I saw right through them. They didn't think I had it in me to be a Syphoner... I sure showed them! Besides, I needed more than what they had to offer. I always felt like the odd man out with my family... but I'm a part of a new family now... a family who cares about me and makes me feel... wanted. I know I made the best choice for myself and I don't think life could possibly get any better than this.

The next day, the restaurant was buzzing with hungry customers ordering their meals. The cooks in the kitchen scrambled eggs and buttered toast, making my mouth water. I was more than ready for the day to be over.

Early afternoon a young woman entered the dining area asking for a table for two. She was cute but not really my type. As I looked around the room, I perceived that I was not the only one who noticed her, almost every male in there was at her beck and call. Moments later, another woman walked in and sat across from her. She was absolutely gorgeous, and her beauty captivated me. I walked over to their table and asked if they'd had a chance to view the menu.

"Can I get the breakfast special? Pancakes, eggs, but can I get turkey bacon instead of the regular one, please?" the effortless beauty said with a smile.

The other girl ordered the same; at least, I think she did. I was too mesmerized by her friend to notice. As I asked them what they'd like to drink, Chuck returned, smiling at customers as they passed him. When the two ladies laid eyes on him, their behaviour changed. They sat up straight and stared at each other wide-eyed. I sensed their discomfort.

"How's the day going so far, Levi?" Chuck asked as he walked behind me.

"It's alright," I replied, feeling sparks of energy once again trickle down my spine. "I'll be right back with your food," I say to the two girls who weren't paying attention. I knew they were waiting for me to leave so they could chat.

I handed their order to a waitress and told her to handle their table. I stood behind a pillar close enough to their table so I could hear what they were saying. This isn't something I normally do, but since overhearing Chuck in his office I've had a bad feeling he's involved in something terrible.

After hearing what they spoke about I knew it was imperative that I reached out to at least one of them. I quickly rung up their orders and jotted down my cellphone number on the back of one of the receipts. Seeing that they ordered the same thing, I figured it wouldn't matter which one I wrote it on. I hope she doesn't freak out about my abrupt approach. I handed the receipt to the girls, and she looked at the back. I held my breath, hoping she wouldn't react in a negative fashion and sure enough, she didn't. She calmly looked at me with concern and curiosity in her eyes. Then she smiled and slipped the note into her pocket for safekeeping. It's hard to tell if she was taken back or used to this sort of thing... I wondered if she would call me. I guess all I can do now is wait and see.

Chapter 7

Sophia

I know Mya was against me following her to meet with Levi, but it's a good thing I did it anyway! I had a front-row seat to everything that took place, and from the way I see it, I have two options: I can leave and let them clean up this mess on their own. It looks like they have everything under control, minus Zohrah's lifeless body lying on the floor. My second option is obvious: I help them. This sort of thing is what I've been trying to avoid my whole life, especially after my last mishap. I have to let them figure things out on their own... its way too risky for me. I can't be exposed. I took a sip from my water bottle, twisted the cap back on, and threw it in my large tote.

Past

The school bell rang, and as always, I waited until the hallway cleared before walking to class. All my teachers were aware as to why I came to class late every day. High school has been a bumpy ride for me, and being the quiet person, I am, I thought I would blend into the background. My shoes echoed against the tiles on the hallway floor as I sped walk to class. Turning the corner, I bumped into Tracy and her friends, they were the "popular" girls in school.

"Oh look, girls, it's the village idiot," Tracy said while the four other girls snickered behind her.

I don't respond.

"What are you wearing, Sophia? You look like you got your clothes from Goodwill. Is that where your mother takes you shopping?" Tracy laughed, barely containing herself.

I once again said nothing and walked past them to get to my class.

After class, I stayed behind as long as possible because I knew the group of girls were out there doing their daily rounds. I could hear their booming laughter as they spoke to others. Boys loved them, and girls wanted to be like them, except me. I enjoyed learning and reading, and I guess they saw me as an outsider because I wasn't a sheep like the rest of the crowd. Eventually, my teacher shooed me out of her class so her other students could get seated. With hesitation, I walked into the hallway with my books in my hand, and the girls were still there. I tried to sneak past them but stopped to take a quick drink at the fountain to quench my thirst. I closed my eyes as the cool water splashed against my mouth; suddenly, I felt a hand push the back of my head, forcing my face into the oncoming flow of water. I dropped my books, gasping for air, and I turned to see Tracy and her friends standing behind me, chuckling. With my dripping face, I bent down to pick up my books and one of the girls reached and slapped them from my hands.

I took a deep breath in.

"What are you going to do about it?" Tracy said as she pushed my shoulder, testing me.

I stood there in disbelief while clenching my fists at my side. My face began to get heated with rage as I watched Tracey standing there with her head high… taunting me. I watched as students turned away with looks of embarrassment on my behalf. Others stood by to observe the show.

"That's what I thought. Now get your ugly face out of my sight," Tracy said, starting to walk away.

"What's your problem with me, Tracy?" I stood tall with my shoulders back and chin up.

"Oh look, everyone, she speaks," she giggled with her friends. Tracy looked around to see who else was watching this performance.

"Oh, I speak all right, and quite well might I add. Not to mention, I'm at the top of all my classes, so the question remains why are you mad? Is it because you only have a pretty face but no brains to go with it? Are you jealous?" I said in the most sarcastic tone I could muster up. The corners of my mouth tugged into a half smile.

"That's all you got? All you have is that you're smarter than me. How the hell could I ever be jealous of the lights of you?" Tracy laughed.

My heart sank as I realized I could never go up against someone like her. Why I even bothered to speak up was beyond me.

"You're talking about brains when look at you. That's ALL you have! You're ugly, your hair isn't even worth mentioning, your outfit look like you got dressed in the dark. Not one single boy here would ever like you… am I right, fellas?" she asked, turning to look at the males who were there listening. They bent their heads in shame, turned away, avoiding eye contact, and some blatantly laughed agreeing with her statement. "Nobody could be jealous of you, you're worthless!" Tracy finally concluded, stepping closer to me. Her words echoed repeatedly in my head… every syllable felt like a punch to my gut.

I scanned the hallway at all the laughing faces. Nobody seemed to pity me, and I could feel my resentment building by the second. My clenched fists started to shake vigorously at my side.

"Aww, look, she's upset," I heard someone say between their chuckling.

Then something inside me erupted

"STOP IT!" I bellowed.

Suddenly, the spout from the drinking fountain flew off, hitting the ceiling. The sounds of laughter stopped immediately. Water sprayed at Tracy and her friends, and their smiles turned into high-pitched squeals as their faces and clothes got drenched with ice-cold water. People in the hall bolted from the scene to avoid getting wet, while others used their hands or books to shield themselves. I raised my hands shielding myself from the water while looking through my fingers in astonishment.

What just happened?

Tracy and her groupies cursed their wet clothes and running makeup. They ran to the bathroom to dry themselves off. Everyone slowly left the dripping hallway, leaving me standing there alone. I took a step forward, and my foot slipped. I crouched down and saw that directly in front of me, where the water fell, was a layer of ice. I picked up a frozen droplet and looked at it closely.

How is this possible?

I stood up and walked around the ice as the school principal came racing around the corner.

"Who did this?" she asked as she saw me trying to tip-toe away. "Sophia Medina, what is the meaning of this?"

"Uhh... I'm not sure what happened," I stammered.

"Hurry up and get to your next class. We'll speak about this at a later date. For now, I need to get this place cleaned up," the principal said sternly.

I sped walk around the icy floor and to my next class. I'm not sure how I'll explain myself out of this one… but I think after today, I won't have much issues with Tracy and her gang of friends.

Present

Walking away from what I saw in the alleyway didn't feel right, but I seriously didn't want to be involved. I've been able to go years undetected by those who hunt us, the Syphoners; I can't just throw that all away. My grandmother told me stories of others out there like us with gifts, but I thought that's all they were… stories. Who was that man in black, and what was he doing to Zohrah? From what I saw, it looked like he was killing her. The way his mouth opened… I've never seen anything like it before. It looked like he was going to swallow her whole. Her legs kicking, trying to get down…I kept replaying it over and over in my mind, and each time, it didn't get easier to digest.

I stopped and turned back to look at my friend Mya.

I recalled seeing the man in black at school earlier today speaking to… I think her name is Karina. It's pretty obvious he's bad news. I can't help but wonder between Mya and Levi, who is the one who was able to put a stop to everything? I want to pretend I didn't see anything, but I can't turn my back on them now; I have to help.

I trek back towards the alleyway. I crept up quietly, neither Levi nor Mya noticed I was there. I saw them both leaning over Zohrah while Levi checked her pulse. Mya is demanding an explanation as to what happened and how he was able to throw Malachi across the alleyway without laying a hand on him.

I guess that answers my question about who has the ability.

Levi is hesitant trying to find the right words to explain him self. He started to tell Mya the truth. Everything in me wanted to scream and shut him up. How could he be so open and trusting to tell anyone about who he really is? But at the same time, Mya has already witnessed something unexplainable. Letting her enter our world now seems like the only right thing to do. I decided to cut him off and reveal myself so he didn't feel alone.

"Hey guys," I said, stepping from behind the shadows.

"Sophia? What are you doing here?" Mya asked suspiciously. "Did you follow me?"

"YES! And it's a good thing I did. I saw everything that happened here!" I said, hoping Mya would understand that I was only trying to help her.

"Everything?" Levi asked.

"Yes. Everything. I saw what you did. I know you have…" I said, trying to reassure him.

"Yo Mya, talk to your friend," Levi said, sounding nervous.

"Ugh, fine! I'll show you. What I'm about to show you can never be spoken of again,"

"Girl…" Mya pointed to the men on the floor behind her. "Now is not the time for speeches!"

I held out my shaky hand and placed the bottle of water in the middle of my palm. We all stared at the bottle intensely. Suddenly, the water started to bubble like it was boiling on a stove. The bubbles started soft but intensified within moments, forcing the cap to pop off and shoot up into the air. I caught the cap as it fell back to the ground and screwed it back on the bottle.

There was silence as we all stared at each other uncomfortably.

"Can someone please explain to me what the hell is going on?" Mya roared, frustrated.

"We have abilities, Mya. And it may be hard to understand now, but I need you to trust me, trust us," said Levi, looking into Mya's eyes.

Mya stared at Levi and I for a moment. I could see the wheels spinning in her head, pondering what she should do next.

"I have so many questions, but we need to get Zohrah out of here," Mya said, breaking the silence. "These guys can wake up at any time," she said.

Levi went over to Zohrah, cradled her in his arms and lifted her frail body.

"Where can we take her?" asked Mya.

"I know just the place. She will be safe there. Trust me," I responded.

"Where?" Mya asked.

"The Underground," I replied as I quickly walked ahead, Mya and Levi followed behind.

Chapter 8

When Sophia said we were going to a place called The Underground, I didn't know what to expect. As we walked through a tunnel leading to this secret place, I could hear water dripping from the ceiling into tiny puddles in the distance. The tunnel was dark, damp and very unnerving. I imagined the Underground to be lacklustre and depressing, but when we finally reached the end of the tunnel, Levi and I watched in admiration. The only way to describe this place was… incredible. It's like a small city, underdeveloped but still very well put together. There were loads of pitched vibrant-coloured tents all over. Pictures, paintings and a large mural went across a large wall across the back wall. The decorative wall art looked beautiful. The mural was filled with different color painted handprints and portraits with smiling faces. There was music and children playing hopscotch; some people were dressed in business suits, while others were dressed in rags. As I observed, one thing stood out to me the most, everyone was happy. There wasn't one frown in sight. Everybody was smiling, which was uplifting because although they didn't have much and basically lived in hiding, they didn't let it steal their joy. As we walked in, many turned to greet us.

"There she is," Sophia pointed to an older woman with silver short curly hair who was talking amongst her friends. The woman saw Sophia approaching and opened her arms wide for an embrace.

"Hola mi dulce nieta!" she said excitedly, holding Sophia's face in her hands and then hugging her tightly again.

"Hola abuela!" Sophia giggled, hugging her back.

Sophia turned to Levi and me.

"Guys, this is my grandma Rosita, grandma Rosita, these are my friends Mya, Levi and ahh…" she said, pointing to Zohrah, who was still out cold in Levi's arms.

"Oh no! what happened to her? Put her down here," Rosita said looking at Zohrah as Levi placed her carefully on a nearby cot. She bent down and brushed Zohrah's hair from her face with her hand to get a better look at her face.

"Ms. Rosita, may I ask why do you guys live here? In The Underground, I mean," I asked, making sure to choose my words carefully.

"Please call me Rosie. We live here, so we can live in peace," she said, looking into my eyes. As I gazed at Rosie, I could tell that she has seen a lot in her lifetime. She witnessed what most couldn't fathom, and because of that, she is wise.

"We live here but there are people that go above ground daily to keep tabs on everything that happens," she continued, "You see over there at those people?" she asked, pointing over to the people dressed in tattered clothing.

"Yes, they look like the homeless people I see on the street," I respond, trying not to stare too much.

"That's right! They only do that to blend in. You couldn't imagine all they hear or see because they are always overlooked and underestimated. And you see those people over there?" she asked, looking towards people in business attire.

"Yes."

"Those people all have different types of jobs, from CEOs to managers to even as simple as a cashier. Everyone here serves a purpose to the bigger picture and plan. They scope out everything, they make connections with as many people as possible, and they keep a look out for anything that may seem suspicious."

"So, all these people live down here but go to work above ground every day?" Levi chimed in.

"That's right," Rosie smiled.

"But why?" I asked, still feeling confused.

"One man, Malachi," she said a little above a whisper.

Levi and I exchange looks, as this is the third time we've heard his name today. Sophia, on the other hand, had no clue.

"Who's that grandma?" Sophia asked.

Rosie bent down and reached inside a box beside Zohrah's cot, and she picked up a large folder. Inside, it held an abundance of photos. Rosie rummaged through the pictures and stopped when she came to the one she was looking for. She pulled out an old, creased photo and handed it to Sophia. In the picture, two men are arm in arm, smiling. One of the men looked identical to Malachi. I grab the picture from Sophia to take a closer look. Yep! It's definitely him.

"He's not bad-looking," Sophia said as we all turned to stare at her. "What!! He has a nice smile!"

"Anyway," I said, ignoring Sophia, "Who is he, and why is he doing this?"

Rosie hesitated, thinking of the best way to answer the question.

"I don't think Malachi himself knows why he does the things he does."

We all stood there silently. A group of women walked by us, one woman with long, beautiful locs stopped abruptly, staring right at me. At first, I wasn't sure who she was looking at, so I turned to see if there was something or someone behind me. The woman continued to stare, her was face frozen like she had seen a ghost. I glared back, starting to wonder if something was wrong. The woman had natural beauty, something you don't see very often in this day and age.

Without makeup, her skin had a natural glow. Something about her felt very familiar, but I had no clue where I knew her. In her eyes, I could see that she recognized me; there was love, compassion and a bit of sadness in them.

"Hi…uh, sorry for staring. My name is Livia. Are you all new here?" she asked.

"They are just visiting," Rosie interrupts. "Their friend here needs our help," she said stepping aside so Zohrah was in clear view.

Livia looked at Zohrah and gasped in horror.

"Is it…?" Livia asks in dismay.

"Yes, he's at it again," Rosie responded.

"I'll get some blankets and pillows to make her more comfortable. It was nice meeting you all," Livia shook our hands and quickly walked away.

I watched her as she walked away. Livia turned back and looked at me, and I could tell there was something more she wanted to say, but whatever it was had to wait. Livia kept walking and disappeared into the crowd. I turned back to Rosie and my friends.

"So, how long have you all been living down here?" Levi asks.

"It's been a very long time, child, years," Rosie sighed.

I couldn't keep pretending that all was well anymore. Everyone seemed happy living here, but I couldn't understand why a multitude of people would play hide and seek with just one man.

"Why don't you guys fight back? There's one of him and all of you!" I blurted out.

"There are others missing, Mya. Almost every week, a few of us disappear," Rosie explained. "The few of us that are here, we need them. We need a lot more than just us if we are going to defeat Malachi. Yes, he is just one man, but he possesses gifts from many, which makes him almost unstoppable."

"But he must have a weakness… right?" I pressed.

'Absolutely! And one day, we will figure out what that is. But for now, we wait and learn."

Hearing the determination in Rosie's voice made me back down. There has to be a way to defeat Malachi, and I know there is!

"Well, guys, it's getting late. Zohrah will be able to get better and build back her strength here. Most importantly, she'll be safe," Sophia said, looking at us all. "I think we should head out. Besides, we still have class tomorrow… right, Mya."

I rolled my eyes at the thought.

"And I have work tomorrow, soooo…" Levi chimed in.

"Well, don't let me keep you back. It was great meeting all of you, and don't be a stranger," Rosie said, giving us all warm hugs.

"I can't thank you enough for doing this, Rosie," I said. "Don't worry, we'll be back soon."

We said our goodbyes and trailed back through the tunnel to enter back to our reality. We waited with Sophia for her uber to arrive, and then Levi and I walked towards the subway station.

"How are you doing with all of this?" he asked.

"It's definitely a lot to take in at once. There's this whole new world that I had no idea even existed. I mean, you and Sophia having…" I stopped myself, not wanting others to hear us as they walked by. "It's just a lot!" I whisper.

"I hear you," he said, thinking for a moment.

"But I still want… need to know more. That's if you're comfortable talking about it."

"I've never shown anyone what I can do, not deliberately anyway. Something about you I know I can trust. There's something different about you, I can feel it." He said, sitting down on a bench while we waited for the train to arrive.

"But you don't know me. How can you be so sure?" I ask, sitting beside him.

"Let's call it a hunch," he shrugged.

"I have so many questions… What is your gift, if you don't mind me asking."

"It's hard to explain," Levi replied, shifting in his seat to face me. "All I know is how I feel. If I am around someone that has a gift, I can feel it, tap into it and I use it for myself."

"So, does the other person know you're stealing their gift?" I inquired.

"I don't think so," Levi said, looking like he'd never thought of that before. "If they knew, I wouldn't have had the chance to save Zohrah."

"Very true," I nod.

We sat and talked for a while not noticing the several trains that passed us.

"So, your name is Mya…"

"Not you asking for my full government name," I laugh and say playfully. "Mya Yu."

He looks at me, taken back and befuddled.

"I'm adopted … so yes, I'm a black girl with the last name Yu."

"True." He replied. "How is it?… being adopted, I mean."

"Mmm… pretty good! My parents are amazing people."

"That's good," he replied. We sat in silence for a little while.

"Some first date, huh," Levi said with a half smile.

"That was a date? Boy, what!" I couldn't help but laugh.

"Did you want it to be?"

I thought for a moment.

"I think there's far too much going on to even think about… dating. Maybe one day we can have a redo."

"We can definitely do that," Levi mocked, checking his watch. "We've been here for over an hour. I think we should get going. I'll follow you home to make sure you get there safely."

"Such a gentleman," I said, batting my eyelashes playfully. "I'm a big girl; you don't have to do that."

"I know I don't have to, but you said it yourself, I'm a gentleman," he said, holding out his arm. "Shall we?"

"Yes, we shall," I reply linking my arm through his.

Chapter 9

Once I returned home from spending time with Levi and the butterflies settled in my stomach, everything that happened earlier that day came back to mind. From finding Zohrah's lifeless body to finding out about Sophia and Levi's gifts, then to top it all off, there's a city of people living right below us that everyone is oblivious to. There's another world that I didn't even know existed, and I can't help but wonder how can I go on with my regular life knowing there are people that need help. Sometimes I question if I didn't go to the club that night to celebrate my birthday, would I be here now? But somehow, I think all this was inescapable, and there's a far bigger depiction than what I'm able to see now.

As Noreen passed my bedroom door, she noticed me sitting at the end of my bed, staring off into space.

"Earth to Mya… what's going on? You look like you had a long day," Noreen said, coming into my room.

"That's one way of putting it. I'm fine, just a lot on my mind."

"You want to talk about it?" Noreen asked.

"It's ok, but thanks, Nor."

Noreen turns to walk back out of my room but stops mid-step.

"You know what, Mya, I am beginning to think you don't consider me your true friend," she said with hurt in her voice.

"What are you talking about?"

"I tell you almost everything. You are one of my best friends. We've been roommates for three years now, and I *still* feel like I don't know much about you. What's up with that?"

"I just don't like burdening people with my issues," I replied, trying to defuse the situation.

"Mya, I wasn't born yesterday. You don't trust me, just admit it!"

"Look, I don't talk to anyone. It has nothing to do with you. So please just drop it," I answered, suppressing my irritation.

"I'm over this. I just hope one day you can open up a little so someone can get to know the *REAL* Mya Yu."

I hate to admit when I'm wrong, but something Noreen said struck a nerve. She was right. She doesn't know much about me, then again, who does? I don't even remember MY own past! If I'm honest, anyone who continuously pries or questions me too much makes me wonder what their motives are. Granted, some people genuinely want to help and be a listening ear. Buts let's face it, those who eagerly want to know things either want to make themselves feel better or talk about you with someone else. And I do not like being the topic of conversation.

After Noreen's rant, she leaves my room, nearly slamming my bedroom door behind her. Too exhausted to chase after her, I leave her alone and decide we'll revisit that conversation at a later date. I lie down and rest my eyes for a second…

The heat from the flames warmed my face. The flames danced as they grew larger by the minute. I couldn't help but think that these are people I once loved, people I once played with and spoke to. Why am I doing this to them? Just then, I felt a soft hand hold mine, I looked up and saw a woman. She crouched down to meet my eyes. Looking at her, I could feel myself start to calm down. Flames started to cease as my anger slowly left. Although I had caused such destruction and turmoil, I could sense the love from her. She didn't judge me like the others; instead, she held me tightly as I sobbed on her shoulder.

"It's okay, my sweet Mya. I'm here now," she said, wiping tears that ran down my cheeks.

"I'm sorry, Mommy, I couldn't control it," I reply between weeps.

"Shhhhh, you don't have to explain to me. But we have to leave here now."

I could see the worry forming in my mother's eyes the longer we stood there. She stood up, and we started to walk away from what used to be our home.

"Why is Daddy doing this?" I asked while we walked.

"I don't know, but we can't risk being caught."

"Where will we go?"

"Somewhere safe. But first, we have to stop and see one of the elders," my mother said, looking down at me. She gave me a half smile. I could tell something was wrong, but knowing my mom had unconditional love for me, my trust could not be shaken.

"Ok, Mommy, let's go," I said, taking her hand.

I opened my eyes, wiping tears before they fell. This time, I didn't wake up frightened or abruptly, this time, my heart felt heavy. The face of the woman in my dream appeared to me again, and I froze. The face I saw was the woman I met earlier today in The Underground, Livia. And I called her … mommy. The tight knot in my throat ached as I tried to contain my emotions. I need answers and fast. I check the time and see that it's almost midnight. I paused for a moment, recalling my 9 a.m. class, and I immediately began to dread the thought of morning. Is sleep more important or my peace of mind? I throw on a pair of thick leggings, a sweater and a jacket as I tip-toe out my bedroom door praying Noreen was asleep. Sure enough, she was wide awake, watching a movie.

"Where are you going?" Noreen asks curiously, getting up from the couch.

"Please, Nor not now," I answer, not in the mood for the third degree.

"Well, you can't just leave without at least letting me know where you're going! What if something happens to you?"

Noreen continued to speak and my aggravation intensified with every word, with every question. I knew she meant well, but at the same time, she was not my mother. I needed her to back off, and I needed her to stop questioning me every chance she had. I wish Noreen would just SHUTUP!

Just then, I noticed Noreen was no longer speaking. In fact, she looked nervous and scared. She traced her fingers along her full lips, but it wouldn't open. She started to scream, but it was muffled because her mouth still would not open. She tried to pry it open with her fingers, she opened her jaw as wide as she could, but her mouth was sealed shut. Starting to panic, Noreen looked at me for help as if I had something to do with this.

"OMG, you're so extra... open your mouth and speak!" I said.

At that moment, Noreen's mouth opened. She felt around her lips with her fingers and glared at me accusingly from the corner of her eyes.

"I have to go. I'll see you later, and don't wait up," I leave and close the door behind me.

The uber drops me off a block away from The Underground tunnel entrance. I didn't want to take any chances in case I was being watched or followed. As I reach the door I look to my left, right and behind me. Once no one was in sight, I knew it was safe to go in.

The past few weeks, I could tell something was different with her. Something shifted, but I just couldn't put my finger on it. She denied anything was going on, but I knew better, she wasn't telling me the truth. Or maybe she doesn't know? Whether she knows or not, tonight was confirmation of what I have been thinking for a while now. You know... I always found it interesting where people look first when they feel like they are being followed; left, right and sometimes behind. How come nobody ever thinks to look up?

Leaning over the ledge of a nearby building, I watch Mya enter the tunnel door leading to The Underground. I pull my phone out of my jeans pocket.

"It's me Noreen...I think I've found her."

Putting the phone back in my pocket, I take a few steps back, giving myself some space to run. I take off sprinting, picking up the pace with every step. I run and step off the ledge, leaping high into the night sky. My frizzy mane around my face unruly, making me feels liberated and free. I jumped from one rooftop to another, running and then springing into the air again and again. I did this until I was out of breath, back outside my bedroom window and in my room.

Chapter 10

The Underground activity died down from when we were there earlier. Children slept soundly on their cots while their parents talked amongst themselves. Walking past some of the chatter, I could hear the nervousness in some of their voices. People looked at me as I walked past them; I searched for the woman I met earlier, the woman in my dream, Livia. I found Zohrah lying on the cot, except now there were pillows and blankets surrounding her. As I stepped closer I could see she was getting better already. Her cheeks were no longer sunken in; her lips were getting back to their full form, and her hair was getting back to its chestnut hue. I was so distracted looking at Zohrah that I didn't even notice a woman was sitting next to her cot on the ground. I lightly tapped the woman's shoulder to get her attention, and sure enough, it was Livia. She jumped, dropping a heap of photos from her hands. I bent down to help Livia gather her pictures, but she scrambled, grabbing them quickly.

"What are you doing here?" Livia asks, tucking the pictures away in a box beside her.

"I need to speak to you."

She looked at me expectantly, giving me her undivided attention.

"The moment I saw you earlier today, I felt an instant connection, it felt like I knew you some how. Then tonight, I had a dream… or nightmare that is still yet to be determined, and you were in it. That's not the first time I've seen you in my dream."

Livia lets out a long sigh and reaches for the box filled with pictures. She looks through the photos, sets some aside then turns back to me.

"Before we get to that, do you mind telling me about your dream?" Livia requests.

I hesitated for a moment because I'd never shared my dream with anyone before, but if I wanted answers, I'd have to trust someone, and my gut said it was her. I told her everything from start to finish, not leaving out a single detail. Livia listens, not daring to make a sound. Certain times, I could see her eyes light up, but then she'd catch herself and play it cool. When I finished explaining everything, I sat down, waiting for Livia to say something. Livia sat quietly for a long time, processing all she just heard. After I got tired of waiting, I broke the silence.

"Well?" I said impatiently.

"Mya, what I'm about to share with you will be a hard pill to swallow. I need you to have an open mind and listen to what I'm saying before jumping to any conclusions. Do you think you can do that?" Livia asked, looking at me in my eyes.

"I'll try," I said in a strong voice but inside my stomach did summersaults.

Livia hands me the cluster of pictures she held in her hands. I took the photographs from her and stared at them carefully, one by one. The first picture was of a woman holding a baby girl and smiling. The adorable infant looked a few months old. She had a toothless smile that could light up a room. The picture made me smile. I flipped through the other photos, and I could see the baby growing up, laughing, standing, taking her first steps and eating with food all over her face. I stopped at one picture with a woman who looked much like Livia with a young girl who reminded me of myself. I took a closer look and the young girl looked exactly like me at maybe 10 or 11 years old. There were several photos of us together. We laughed, made silly faces and did the peace sign with our fingers.

"Is this me?" I finally asked Livia, pointing to the picture.

"Yes, that's you," she replied, looking at the picture as if recalling the fond memories.

How could this be possible? Unexpectedly, I flashback, and I hear myself say, "Ok, mommy."

"In my dream, I called you mommy. Livia, are you my biological mother?"

She paused before answering.

"Yes, I am."

We both sit in silence for a moment.

"I know it's hard to believe, but it's true. When you were 11 years old, I placed you with a family where I knew you'd be safe. Where I knew no one could find you," she said close to a whisper.

"Safe from who?" I inquired.

"His name is Malachi."

Hearing his name again instantly made me furious. I began to gather my things to leave.

"Where are you going?" Livia asked in a panic.

"You mean to tell me I was sent away from you… my mother… because of this Malachi guy?" I ask, standing over her.

"It's not that simple," Livia replies.

"It just seems like Malachi is the common denominator. I'm going to end this for good. I'm *NOT* scared of him!" I lash out.

I turn on my heels to walk away, but Livia spins me back around quickly to face her.

"You can't just go after him! If it were that easy, do you think we would be in this mess? THINK Mya!" Livia said, matching my tone. "Malachi is extremely powerful."

When she said that, I instantly recalled my discussion with Rosie, saying how formidable Malachi is.

"He has an ability," I finally retorted, sitting back down.

"He has countless. He's been stealing abilities from innocent people for years."

"Is that what happened to Zohrah?"

"Exactly."

"So, what does any of this have to do with me? What does he want?"

"He wants you to be apart of his army and stand by his side, Mya. He wants YOU," Livia said, looking at me, wondering exactly how much I knew.

"On his side? How the hell could I help him?" I asked, confused out of my mind.

Livia stared at me then she understood why I was so confused.

"You don't know, do you? You haven't figured it out yet?" Livia said but it seemed more of a question for herself than me.

"Know WHAT????" I yelled, no longer able to hide my impatience.

"Mya, you also have a gift. In fact, with dedication and practice, you would and could be thee most powerful person in our people's existence. If Malachi was to have you on his side, you two would be unstoppable."

Breathe, Mya, I reminded myself.

"I have a gift? I HAVE AN ABILITY???!!!" I can't help but scream as I felt irritation and confusion wash over me. "What does this mean? Am I not human? Am I a mutant like the X-Men?" I exclaim, pacing the floor.

"Try to calm down", Livia tries to reason with me.

"What do you mean, calm down," I bellow, forgetting Zohrah was resting beside us. "*THIS* is me being *CALM*!!"

Livia lunges at me to cover my mouth.

"Shhhhh!! I said in the beginning to have an open mind. I understand this is difficult to hear and process, but this is how life is sometimes. Right now, the best thing for you to do is to be strong and listen," Livia said, slowly removing her hand from my mouth.

Zohrah began to stir and suddenly tried to sit up in the cot and started screaming. Her eyes darted around the room in fear; she looked disoriented and weak. She attempted to get up while mumbling something; I was only able to understand a few words of what she was saying.

"Where am I? I want to go home! Let me go home!" she repeated over and over.

Livia immediately went over to Zohrah and began to calm her down. Livia quickly brushed her hands across Zohrah's face, and instantly there was a significant change in her demeanor; she became somber and at peace.

"You are okay, Zohrah, everything is fine… shhh, be still," Livia whispered softly.

"I'm okay, everything is fine… shhh," Zohrah repeated.

"Go to sleep," Livia said.

Zohrah once again repeated what she said as she lay back down to rest.

I gazed, astonished, wondering how Livia was able to calm her down so quickly. Zohrah seemed hypnotized in a way. We sat in silence for a while. I still have to process the thought of having abilities and that Livia is my birth mother. But I needed to know what just happened.

"What was that about?" I asked.

"She's been doing that every so often… she'll wake up confused because…"

"Not that! What you just did there. How did you do that?" I probed, pointing towards Zohrah.

"Oh… I'm what they call a Tranquilist. I'm able to inflict emotion on people without them realizing it's not them or their desires to feel that way," she stated.

"A Tranquilist? Like tranquility? So no matter how a person is feeling you can make them feel something else?" I question.

"That's correct," Livia nodded.

"What if you wanted someone to feel another emotion like anger or… pain?"

"Why would I want that?" Livia asked as she cocked her head to one side.

I don't answer her…this is a lot to digest. Livia took this opportunity to get back to what we were speaking of before.

"You had no idea you were different? There were no occurrences where you thought something was strange?" Livia asks, breaking the awkward silence.

I recalled all the times when things happened where I thought it was strange, for instance, in the class room when everyone turned around at the same time, also getting into the nightclub without waiting in line, but the one that stood out most to me was with Noreen when she couldn't open her mouth to speak. All of these things happened with a simple thought of me saying what I wanted, but I thought it was all coincidence… is there no such thing as coincidence now? I looked towards Livia, this beautiful woman who is my mother and I could see the resemblance between us. But there is one thing for sure: I know we differ. I would never in a million years send away my own child, no matter what the circumstances were.

"Can I ask you a question?" I asked Livia, turning to look directly into her eyes.

"Anything."

"I know you say you sent me away to be safe from Malachi, but didn't you think for one moment that staying with you may have been best for me? To learn more about myself and our people?"

"I did think about that, but for me, it was more important at the time to keep you safe. I saw the opportunity for you to live a normal childhood with a family that could care for you, and I took it. I wanted you to somehow retrieve your innocence."

"You call reoccurring nightmares and being able to control what people do with a single thought being normal?" I chuckled at the thought.

"About those nightmares…"

"There's more?" I asked, trying not to let my irritation show.

"Those nightmares you keep having aren't exactly nightmares at all. They are suppressed memories."

"So there really was a fire… and I was the cause of it? Is that what you're saying right now?"

"I wouldn't place all the blame on you, but that is what happened."

"Next, you'll probably say that my father is really Voldemort," I said bringing my knees close to my chest as I rocked back and forth.

I know I should have told Mya the whole truth but, how could I? She had to withstand so much in one night already that I couldn't bring myself to tell her more. There's so much more to this story she doesn't know yet, and I'm afraid she won't understand. The Elders... her father... where would I begin? Not to mention her abilities... she could barely handle the thought of having one ability... how am I supposed to tell her that she was born blessed with TWO – making her a Doppel Paladin. Her reaction alone proved she wasn't ready to receive that information. I should have told her everything... in time, I will. All I can do is pray she forgives me for keeping secrets from her and hope she doesn't find out elsewhere before I have the chance to tell her myself. She will have to realize that I meant no harm and that I love her; after all, I am her mother.

<div align="center">~~~</div>

Where am I? How did I get here? The last thing I remember is I was arguing with Karina, and then... those men came an..., and he took m...my... he sucked it right out of me. I remember the excruciating pain and the sound of my skin tearing apart. I want to go home, but I can barely move. I want to go home; let me go home! Wait... Do you feel that? What's touching my face? It's so soft and so pacifying. Do you hear that sound? It sounds like… humming… a melody. Who's humming? It sounds so beautiful I don't want it to stop, please don't stop. I'm okay… everything is going to be fine… shhhh. I think I'm going to rest here for a wh…

Chapter 11

By the time I got home, it was almost 3 AM and I set my alarm to wake up in a few hours for class. My head was swarming with thoughts I couldn't get past; it made me question my whole existence. Does this mean my whole life was a lie? I remembered the déjà vu that happened while in class, the first time I met Zohrah. Could that instance be a part of my ability? And does this mean I should practice using my gift? How many others are there that are like me? The list goes on. I go to my room and lie down, hoping to stop the tornado spinning through my brain. In no time at all, I drifted into a deep slumber, and for the first time in a while, there was no nightmare to wake me up.

A few hours later, Noreen woke me up.

"Mya! Mya!!" Noreen whispered loudly.

"Whaaaat," I groan, feeling groggy.

"Can I come in?"

"Mmmmhm," I mumbled, rolling over to see her in my doorway.

Noreen comes in and sits at the end of my bed.

"Sorry to wake you. I just wanted to speak to you quickly before I head out. You interested in a girl's night tonight? You've seemed super stressed lately, and I think it's well-deserved. Are you in?" she asked.

"I thought you were mad at me," I reply.

"You know I don't stay mad for long. So you down?"

"Sure, I'm down."

"Perfect! Invite your friend Sophia, she's a good time! So I'll see you at home later tonight."

"Sounds good. Noreen, wait," I said before she left my room. "I'm sorry for…"

"No need," Noreen waved, cutting me off. "We're good. Oh, and by the way… you look exhausted."

Noreen left my room, I tossed and turned, trying to fall back asleep as I had a half hour left before my alarm would sound, but I was unsuccessful. My body was exhausted, but my mind was on autopilot, I couldn't get last night's conversation with Li... my mother, out of my head. I check the time on my phone and notice I have a missed text message from Levi.

Levi: Hey, What you sayin' tonight?
Mya: Hey! I'm going out with my girls tonight.
Levi: Ok, cool. If anything changes, let me know.
(Mya liked his msg)

I put my phone on my nightstand and roll out of bed to get myself ready for class. I take a hot shower, take my braids out allowing my mane to be free. Apply some mascara and lip gloss to help spruce myself up a little. By the time I was ready, I realized I was going to be late for Mr. Henry's class and knowing him, and he would use me as an example of what not to do… again. As predicted, I got to class late. I open the door slowly, making sure not to create even the smallest sound, and I sneak and sit at the back of the class. He looks up and sees me sneaking in. *Please don't call me out again,* I thought to myself. To my surprise, he looks at me and goes to open his mouth to say something, but nothing comes out. I could see in his eyes that he was just as surprised as I was. No one in class noticed Mr. Henry's look of confusion, all except Sophia, of course. She turned to her side and glanced to see what had Mr. Henry acting so bizarre, Sophia and I made eye contact. Finally, Mr. Henry gave up and continued with his lesson. I sighed with relief but couldn't help but hear my mother's voice asking,

"So, you had no idea you were different? There were no occurrences where you thought something was strange?"

I ignored my intuition and tried to concentrate for the rest of the class.

After class, I gathered my things quickly and left. Sophia caught up with me in the hallway.

"You look terrible. Lack of sleep much?" Sophia commented.

"Gee, thanks, Sophia; you really know how to make a girl feel special," I say sarcastically. "I had a very eventful night."

"Really? Please do tell! Were there boys invol…"

"Hi… uh, Mya, can we talk?" Karina stopped Sophia and I in our tracks.

"You've got to be kidding me," Sophia snorts. "Haven't you done enough?"

"You've got two minutes, Karina," I replied feeling curious to hear what she had to say.

"I just want you to know that I wasn't aware everything was going to happen the way it did," she said quickly and quietly. "I never would have agreed to…"

"Yea, well, you did! You sold out your best friend… who does that?" Sophia spat, unable to bite her tongue.

"Sophia… let her finish," I say, feeling Sophia's glare burning the side of my head.

"I was wrong… so so wrong. Please tell Zohrah I'm sorry. Please," Karina pleaded. "How is she? Where is she?"

"Pfff, none of your…"

"She's fine," I cut off Sophia again before she's able to finish. "And of course, you must know I'd never tell you where she is… that's just common sense."

We stand there awkwardly, staring at each other.

"Thank you for listening to me. And please, if you need anything… if Zohrah needs anything," Karina says.

"Girl, now you damn well know that won't be happening… respectfully," I say, shutting down her offer.

Karina scurries away, looking defeated.

"BYE! Pff," Sophia says loud enough for her to hear. "The nerve of that girl, right? Ugh!"

I don't respond instead, I keep walking.

"What were we talking about before we were rudely interrupted?" Sophia continued. "Oh right, you were about to tell me about your date last night," she grinned.

"Date?" I choke. "I wish… I went back to the underground last night and basically had the rug pulled from underneath me."

"Wait, back up, you went back there? Why?" Sophia asked, confused.

I thought for a moment if I should tell Sophia the truth. Could I trust her? My whole life, as I know it, has been a lie, so who can I trust but myself? I looked at my friend, and although I had these doubts, I had to take a leap of faith. As Sophia and I walked to the bus stop outside, I explained everything to her. I told her about my dream. This is what led me to go looking for answers in The Underground. Of course, I conveniently left out the part about me starting that fire, I don't need my friend believing I'm an arsonist on top of everything else going on. I told Sophia about the conversation I had with Livia about her being my biological mother. Saying it out loud sounded unreal. I shared about having abilities, and the strange occurrences that I believed happened because of my power. From outside the club the first night, we hung out to the confrontation with Noreen the night before. Sophia listened intently, not saying a word. When I was through, she was extremely supportive and understanding.

"Firstly, I just want to say that I'm sorry you had to endure this all by yourself. Had I known anything like this was happening, I would have been there for you in a heartbeat," Sophia said, patting my arm.

"It's ok, but thanks. I'm just glad I have someone to talk to about this. Seeing that you trusted me enough to show me your true self I figured the least I could do is return the favour."

"Well, I'm glad you told me," Sophia nudged me as we reached the bus stop. "So now tell me more about this ability of yours. Have you taken it for a test drive?"

"Of course not! I can't do it just like that. What if people notice?" I say, looking around nervously.

"People are way too narcissistic to notice a thing. Look around, people don't even make eye contact anymore," Sophia said looking at the people who were either texting and walking, talking on their phone or taking selfies.

I take notice of what she's saying and realize she's absolutely right. Things can happen right before someone's eyes and nobody would notice unless it popped up in an app. Sophia then takes out a half drank water bottle from her purse, and she stares at the bottle.

"What are you doing?" I whisper.

"Shh, just look!"

Sophia continues to concentrate on the water bottle. Suddenly, the liquid in the bottle starts to spin, making a tiny cyclone. The cap of the bottle flew high into the air, and waterspouts up into the air and sprays towards me. I jump out of the way just in time, but instead of a splash like I'm expecting to hear, I hear something hard hit the ground. I look, and ice pellets are scattered around me.

"You can change the water temperature?"

"Yep! I'm still working on it, but it's pretty cool, huh?" Sophia smiled innocently.

"Definitely! Well, I'll work on mine another time, I guess."

"No, Mya, do something now," Sophia urges as we enter onto the bus. "It doesn't have to be anything big."

"Right now, with all these people here?" I look around at the crowd on the bus.

"Why not?"

I couldn't think of a reason why not to. I would never think of anything for people to do that's dangerous or that may hurt others. I thought long and hard, and I had no idea what I could do. Some high school students entered the bus with their backpacks, bumping everyone as they passed. Another young female wearing heels passed by, stepping on my foot with her heel. I winced in pain, and she didn't even look back to see who she stepped on or to apologize. I cannot stand crowded buses; that gave me the perfect idea.

"Well?" Sophia asked, waiting for me to do something.

I ignored her and closed my eyes to concentrate on my thoughts. Although in the past I've never had to close my eyes, let alone concentrate, to make something happen, for some reason, it seemed necessary this time around. I thought about what I wanted a few times, and when I was finished, I opened my eyes and waited. At the next stop, everyone on the bus got up unanimously and headed for the exits. The bus driver looked around as every person on his bus got off at the same stop, all except Sophia and myself. Sophia looked around with her eyes wide like saucers.

"This is a first. I guess I'm your personal driver today, ladies," said the driver, looking at us in his review mirror.

I turned and giggled at Sophia.

"What was that?" Sophia asked.

"I thought it would be nice to have a private bus ride home," I beamed.

"Now that's what I'm talking about! That's my girl!" Sophia nudged me, then stretched out along two vacant seats.

For the rest of the ride, no one else got on our bus. We sat, talked and laughed. I invited her to girl's night and she agreed to come but had doubts about the whole ordeal.

"Are you sure it's a good idea to go out with Noreen after that whole 'mouth wide shut' thing?" Sophia asked curiously.

"Well, considering she's not Tom Cruise, I'm sure it's all forgotten. Personally, I'd rather hang out and keep it low-key tonight, but I already told her I'd go. So, for sure, you're coming, right?"

"I wouldn't miss it," she stands and rings the bell as her stop approaches. "So I'll pick you guys up at, say, 10? See you then, and keep practising," she winked.

I waved at her as she got off the bus.

Chapter 12

When I got home, the apartment was dark, and Noreen wasn't back yet. It was still early, so I decided to turn on the TV in my room to catch up on some shows I'd missed. I figured I'd shower in a couple of hours and get ready then.

I could hear music pumping, and I felt it vibrating through my chest. I looked around, and it appeared to be I was in a nightclub. Lights are flickering as people dance to the beat. I scanned the room, wondering how I got here in the first place because, last I remembered, I was in my room. I started to move to the music without even thinking, suddenly, I saw Mr. Chuck Purnell, Levi's boss; he was looking in my direction. I turn my back to Mr. Purnell and Mr. Henry is standing right in front of me with a grin. His smile wasn't his ordinary smile either; it looked evil in a way. For whatever reason I felt uneasy and the need to run. However, I stood there frozen as goose bumps covered my skin. Screams filled my ears; I turned to see Sophia being held by…

I jolt out of my bed, unsure of where I was at first; the bright light and background laughter from the comedy airing on TV was an instant reminder. I must have fallen asleep. I get up and go into the kitchen to get a drink. Noreen was sitting on the couch in the living room, texting away while a movie played on our large flat screen.

"Hey," she said, not looking up from her phone. "I didn't want to wake you, and you looked exhausted this morning."

"Yea, I must have dozed off for a bit."

"Tonight is still a go, right? I mean, you're not too tired, are you?" Noreen asked, finally looking up.

"I'll be ok. We're still on. Sophia is coming too. She said she can pick us up at 10 p.m."

"Perfect! We're going to have a blast," Noreen sounded relieved. "You can sleep in tomorrow or for the rest of the weekend if you like."

Deep down, I was not in the mood to go anywhere, and the closer time got, the stronger that feeling of indifference became. I dragged my feet back to my room to pick out what to wear. I decided to go with something simple yet elegant, nothing over the top and something comfortable. I chose black-distressed jeans and a low-back bodysuit. I fluffed my fro and refreshed my edges. I threw on my chunky heel black booties, added some color to my lips for a little pizazz, and I was ready to go. I took one last glance at myself in the mirror before we left. I still couldn't shake that "this is a bad idea" feeling from the pit of my stomach, but I threw a smile on my face instead.

We pulled up to Club 6IX, and the feeling of dread consumed me, but once we were inside, the club was alive with pulsing music and neon lights flashing in sync with the bass. Noreen headed straight to the bar to get us all the drinks. The air was thick with the scent of sweat and perfume. Sophia smiled ear to ear with excitement; I tried to join in but still couldn't get past my feeling of disconcertment. Mr. Henry's smiling face flashed in my thoughts.

"You okay?" Sophia asked.

"I'm not sure. I just have this weird feeling that we shouldn't be here," I admit.

"Ok, listen, we'll stay for a while, have a drink or two, enjoy the music, and if you feel like this in an hour still, I'll make up something to get us home. Deal?"

"You said the same thing to me the first time we came here for my birthday" I recall feeling touched.

"Well, what are friends for? We've come a long way since that night… now let's go!"

Sophia pulled me by my arm to the dance floor. Right away, men gathered around her as she moved her hips to the song and sang along with the melody. Realizing there were no prospects in which I'd be in the least bit interested, I closed my eyes and danced allowing myself to relish in the moment. Noreen found us on the dance floor and handed Sophia and I our drinks. I could tell Noreen had a few drinks before coming to find us, but there was something else. I looked closely at Noreen, her forehead glistened with sweat, granted, it is hot in here, but we haven't been in here that long. She was also unusually quiet. The Noreen I know always had something to say.

"Hey!" I nudged her. "You alright?"

"Me? Yea, I'm fine, of course!" she smiled while her eyes darted left to right. I knew then she was not telling the truth, but I left it alone.

"I'm going back to the bar," Noreen said without giving me time to protest.

Within minutes, Noreen was lost in the crowd again. Deciding not to go after her, I downed my drink, and it was delicious. I danced and pushed any ill feelings I had towards tonight from my mind, and the night may end up going better than I thought. Moments later, I began to feel strange, everything around me moved in slow motion, which was impossible. I couldn't be drunk already. Putting my hands to my face, I shook my head to try and get the uneasiness to leave. I started to lose balance, and my knees buckled slightly underneath me. I look up to my left, and through the crowd, I see someone who strongly resembles Mr. Chuck Purnell, Levi's boss. He was looking in my direction. I must be seeing things. I thought it was my imagination until I felt the prickle of his gaze as our eyes locked. He started walking towards us. Sophia stopped dancing and came over to me.

"What's wrong?" Sophia asks.

Before I'm able to answer, Chuck is standing right behind her. He gripped Sophia's arm, causing her to jump when she saw his face and snatched her arm from his grasp. The crowd around continued to dance, oblivious to the tension. Chuck lunged at us, but we sidestepped, using the crowd to our advantage. He missstepped and slipped on the wet floor. We backed away from him, allowing the crowd to come between us. Seeing this as our opportunity to escape, we ran but bumped right into Mr. Henry, who peered at us with a cunning smile. Sophia and I looked at each other; we knew he couldn't chase us both. Sophia ran while Mr. Henry charged at me. My stomach leaped to my throat in fear as I backed away from him. He gripped my arm but I twisted it from his grasp. I shook my head, fighting the feeling of intoxication. The crowd pushed us around as the music quickened. He got frustrated, pushed people out of the way and came at me quickly. He struck first, he aimed a punch at my abdomen, but I blocked it with my forearm. I retaliated with a swift kick to the shin, he grunted but did not falter. He looked at me in shock, and to be honest, I shocked myself. He countered with a backhanded strike that I was able to avoid. Almost like I was able to anticipate his next move. I sensed a shift in his strategy. He was no longer trying to overpower me but out-think me instead. I scanned the room quickly, suddenly remembering Noreen, but she was nowhere to be found. Maybe she made a run for it. I shook my head to make the room stop spiralling. My vision started getting blurry, and I put my hand to my forehead, trying to see where Sophia went so we could get out of there. Screams filled my ears of a familiar voice. Behind me, Sophia yelled for me to run while Malachi stood behind her, holding her close. I didn't want to believe what I was seeing, but having a clear view of the tattoo on his arm, I knew for sure it was him. I tried to get myself together because if there was any time I needed to use my gift, it was now.

"Everybody sto…."

The bottle crashed over my head, sending glass flying. The crowd screamed and hurried for the exits. My vision blurred, and I collapsed to the wet floor, unconscious.

Chapter 13

I woke up with a throbbing headache. I tried to open my eyes, but my eyelids felt too heavy, and I found myself drifting back und…

I groaned, trying to move slightly. Again, my eyes fluttered but refused to open all the way. Where am I, and why do I feel like this? My head pounded with every move…

I heard muffled talking and whispers. Is someone calling my name? Where am I? I go to move my arms but can't due to my hands being tied behind my back. I feel panic and fear rise in me, choking me, preventing me from speaking, screaming. I feel my body going back under. I try to fight the darkness from coming, but I ca…

My eyes shoot open, and I look around the dark, familiar room. I'm lying on a couch; I scan the room. I'm in my living room at home, but I know I'm not safe. Why can't I move? My hands are tied behind me, and my feet are tied, too. Is this real? I look down and see that I'm still dressed in my clothes I picked out earlier. I hear movement from across the living room; I look up to see Sophia sitting on the floor facing me, leaning against the wall. She's struggling with the ropes that are around her wrists and ankles.

"Sophia?" I whisper.

Sophia looked up at me.

"Oh my gosh, you're awake! I was so worried. Are you ok?" Sophia asked.

The sight of Sophia forced my eyes wide open. She didn't look like her usually well-put-together self. Her hair was dishevelled, makeup was smeared, and her eyes were bloodshot red.

"Have you been crying?" I asked.

"I've been worried!" she replied, fighting with the ropes holding her ankles and wrists together.

"What happened? Where's Noreen?" I asked.

"We were set up *that's* what happened! No one will tell me anything."

"But we're in my apartment," I said, looking around. "Noreen has to be here. Or maybe she saw what was happening and went to get help."

"I doubt it. The thing is, Mya… Noreen…"

A male voice interrupted Sophia before she had the chance to finish.

"Oh good, you're up! I was starting to worry," Malachi walked slowly from the hallway into the living room.

His boots knocked against the hardwood floor with every step he took, Mr. Henry and Chuck stood on either side of him. This was my first-time coming face to face with the infamous Malachi; he looks exactly like the photos I saw of him a few nights ago. Strange that he hasn't aged at all, not even one strand of grey hair on his head. I stare at him, and he stares back at me. Malachi looked nothing like I anticipated; I expected to see evil, hatred, anger and a man with inner demons fighting to come out. Instead, I saw a man with hurt, pain and love in his eyes. Maybe even a hint of recognition? He had the same look Livia had when she saw me in The Underground. I quickly turned away, forcing my mother out of my head.

"Now, let's get acquainted, shall we? My name is…"

"I know who you are, so you can cut the shit, tell me why I'm here and what you and your lackeys want with us," I said, cutting him off.

"She's feisty," Malachi says to Mr. Henry. "You didn't tell me she was a little firecracker. I must say, Mya, I'm impressed," he turns back to me.

"If you think that's impressive, untie my hands so you can see what else I can do," I said remembering what I'm capable of. A flash of the city up in flames resurfaces in my memory.

"You remind me so much of myself. Granted, you look more like your mother, which is a good thing, might I add, but on the inside, you're all me. I can see it in your eyes," Malachi said, leaning in and making eye contact with me.

"Ok, first off, I'll never be like you! Secondly, what does my mother have to do with any of this?" I asked.

Malachi squints at me for a moment then it dawns on him.

"Oh, did mommy dearest not tell you when you visited her in The Underground the other night? And before you ask, yes, I know you saw her, and yes, I know about The Underground because I know all, see all and hear all. I have eyes and ears everywhere, sweetheart, always remember that."

"Tell me what?"

"You guys will want to see this," he said to Mr. Henry and Chuck.

Malachi crouched down and came face to face with me.

"Mya… I am your father. Livia, your mother… is my wife."

That caught my attention; my posture straightened as I heard the words come from his mouth. I saw Sophia lean over and peek at me from behind Malachi. Mr. Henry and Chuck shift uncomfortably, and they do not look happy about this at all. Malachi looked around to everyone's blank stare.

"That's right, you all heard correctly. I'm Mya's daddy!" he smiles.

"LIAR!!" I yell.

"Oh, but it's true, my dear."

How could this be possible? Why didn't Livia tell me this before?

"If what you say is true, then prove it," I say through my gritted teeth.

"I might be a power-hungry prick, but one thing I am not is a liar," Malachi replies, trying to avoid my request.

"I. Said. PROVE IT!" I scream.

"The fire," he answers, realizing I won't let this go.

"Everybody seems to know about the fire I started. That proves nothing."

"Wait, that was *you*?" Sophia interrupts. "I thought that was just a rumour…"

"You!" he turns to Sophia, cutting her off mid-sentence. "No talking."

She mocks him and screws up her face at him.

"Anyway, as I was saying, yes, everyone knows about the fire. However, no one knows why it started," he continued.

"Well… tell me then."

He paused and sighed for a moment; he looked like he was recalling a painful memory. Although I was angry, a very small part of me felt almost sorry for him. Maybe he's not the evil man that everyone thinks he is. After taking a moment to collect his thoughts, he turned to me to tell me his version of what happened.

"You were 11-years-old. You were so innocent and young. You were the apple of my eye," he smiled, recalling the love he once felt. "I started getting into some heavy stuff that many didn't approve of, especially your mother."

"What kind of stuff?" I questioned, refusing to let any details slip through the cracks.

"I was stealing power from others. I became someone I myself did not recognize but I couldn't stop. I can't stop."

"Why not?"

"Using your power too much can become addictive like a drug. Not everyone struggles with this issue, but I most certainly do."

"You couldn't even stop for your own daughter?"

"It's not that easy! If I could, I would. Even using your own ability, a great deal can cause you to become consumed; of course, it's worse for some than others. Our people would only use their power when absolutely necessary which is how our people were able to hide in plain sight so well.."

Mr. Henry and Chuck stand like statues behind Malachi in silence. Sophia stares at Malachi unsure whether to believe what he's saying or not.

"I'm a different person now. I can't go back to how things were," he continued.

"That's not true," I said softly, hoping to get through to him. "You can make your own choices. People make mistakes!"

Malachi was silent then he sat on the couch beside me.

"Who did I catch you stealing power from?" I asked.

"My brother Michael."

For the first time, we all saw a different side to him, remorse. Once again, a piece of my heart broke for him.

Suddenly, memories flooded my mind. My father left home without saying goodbye, so I followed him to see why. I tracked him to a wooded area filled with large trees; he had one man with him, and two others were already there waiting. I stood peeking behind a tree as I saw Malachi pick up the man by his neck. I squinted to see who the man was, and sure enough, it was my Uncle Michael. He looked nervous and shocked, but there was something else I was detecting, but I couldn't figure it out. He was fighting to get away, but nothing loosened Malachi's grip. He opened his mouth and started to inhale my uncle's power. Much like Zohrah, my uncle shrunk, shrivelled and looked old. His clothes hung against his skin and bone. When Malachi was satisfied, he dropped him. My uncle shrieked out in pain as he fell to the floor. I flinched, hearing his brittle bones crack as he hit the dirt ground. I didn't understand what was happening or why Daddy was acting strange.

"Daddy?" I said in a small voice, stepping out from behind a tree.

"Mya? Mya sweetie, what are you doing here?" Malachi said looking around nervously as if wondering how much I'd seen.

He tries to come to me and I back away from his reach.

"What is wrong with Uncle Mike? What have you done?" I asked.

"He's fine, sweetheart, see! Michael, get up and show Mya that you're fine," he demands.

Michael rolls around and groans in agony. The two men with him bend down and help Michael to stand up. I saw the faces of the men, and neither of them looked familiar. I look at my Uncle Mike and he looks tattered, vulnerable and wounded. Instantly, I knew he was not ok.

"You did this! You hurt him!" I boomed. "You're a bad man, daddy! A horrible man!" I turned and sprinted back towards town with tears flowing down my cheeks.

"Mya, wait!" Malachi called after me, but I kept running.

I'm dragged back to reality, breathing heavily. I looked straight into Malachi's eyes, and any feeling of love or sympathy I felt moments ago was depleted.

"You act like you feel bad, but you were smiling during the whole thing. I remember what you did, I saw and heard everything, and *you* enjoyed it! I don't know how I thought even for a *second* that a weak, power-hungry, pretentious, pathetic coward like you had a heart!" I spat. "I want nothing to do with you!"

Malachi stood up and signalled Henry, who then pulled out a handgun with a silencer at the end.

"The thing is, Mya, I really don't care about what you think or want… actually, that's a lie, I do, but it's obvious you won't make this easy, so let's get back to the question you asked me earlier, I believe it was 'what do *I* want?" he walks back towards me. "My answer is I want *you*. I want you to join me, get to know me and possibly trust me again. I want to make up for the years I've missed. And in the end, I want you and your power on my side," he said, tapping my nose with his index finger. I move my face away.

"I'll never join you and your minions!"

"See, I knew you'd say that, so of course, I thought of a plan B."

Mr. Henry walks over to Sophia and puts the gun to her forehead. Sophia quivers in fear but doesn't let the terror show on her face. She clenched her jaw as tears welled up in her eyes, but she refused to let them fall.

"Don't do it, Mya," Sophia whispers.

I stare at Sophia, feeling torn.

"So, what will it be, Mya?" Malachi asks. "You can come with me, give me a chance, and your friend lives. You don't, and… well, you're a smart girl. You can figure it out."

I stare at Malachi angrily. I glance towards Mr. Henry, and he places his finger gently on the trigger. In my mind, I go through a list of scenarios to get out of this mess. Malachi is more powerful than both Sophia and I put together not to mention no one here knows that Sophia has abilities. The less Malachi knows, the better. Then there are his two puppets who have abilities, which would make it three men against two young females. Feeling sick to my stomach, I knew what I had to do.

"I'll go," I say quietly.

"I'm sorry I didn't catch that," Malachi said sarcastically.

"You heard me; now let her go."

"Attah girl."

Mr. Henry puts the gun away as Chuck unties Sophia, and she stands rubbing her wrists.

"I'll be ok… go… we'll talk later," I said, holding back tears and forcing a smile.

"That's right, Sophia, you'll see her at school bright and early Monday morning. What kind of father would I be if I deprived Mya of her education?" Malachi said.

She glares at Malachi and turns back to me.

"Take care of yourself," she walks to the door.

"Hey, feel free to come over once Mya is settled. Mi casa es su casa," he says to Sophia.

"Estas loco!" she yelled loudly, leaving the apartment.

"I like her," Malachi laughs as he unties me.

"Alright, we should go get you settled into your new home."

"I need to pack."

"Nonsense, I'll send one of my men to grab your things," he says.

"You mean you have more lackeys?" I ask.

Ignoring me, Malachi makes a quick phone call.

"Send someone to pick up both of my daughter's things and have them by my house. Yes, tonight.

Perfect I'll text you the address," he hands the phone to Chuck.

"Did you say BOTH daughters?" I ask, confused.

"Sweetie, come along now we're leaving," he called out.

Before I had the chance to realize he wasn't speaking to me, Noreen stepped into the hallway.

"Took you long enough," Noreen replied, giving Malachi a warm hug.

I stood there frozen in disbelief. All this time Noreen has been lying to me? Was this her agenda all along? Is this why she always questioned me about what I was doing and where I was going? I thought she genuinely wanted to know me as a person when the truth is she just wanted to report back to Malachi, *our* father. Wait, if he's her father, that makes her… my half-sister! Everyone I thought meant something to me had been lying to me, and my stomach turned at the thought. A flash of Noreen running as the fire surrounded her in the town resurfaced. That's why she was in my dream… or suppressed memory.

"I believe you already know each other," he said, looking at the both of us.

I stood glaring at Noreen, not daring to say a word; you could cut the tension with a knife. Noreen extended her hand out for a handshake.

"OMG, it feels so good to finally tell you the truth… I was an only child for so long…or so I thought… I mean, I had friends and my best friend Dan…"

"You knew who I was all this time?" I asked, cutting her off.

"Well, no, but the other night when my mouth was sealed shut because you said to stop talking… that basically confirmed any suspicion I had," she explained.

I took a step towards Noreen as my hands shook slightly with rage.

"Let's make something clear. You and me… we're NOT family, so do me a favour and stay out of my way!" I say clenching my fists at my side.

Noreen straightens her posture and smiles, but not the sweet smile I've always known.

"I have a better idea," she smirked. Noreen pointed at me with her index finger, and my body flew to the side and slammed into the wall. "Stay out of *my* way! You're not the only one with tricks up their sleeve. Watch how you talk to me."

Noreen storms off, and I stand up, dusting my clothes off.

"Nice going, *Dad!*" I say sarcastically, then leave.

Malachi sighs to himself and shakes his head.

"This should be fun!" he says to Mr. Henry and Chuck as they both look at him dumbfounded. "C'mon, lackeys, let's go!"

~~~

I never thought this day would come… the prodigal daughter has returned. I couldn't be happier with our union, although it's nothing like I would have imagined it. The night Noreen called me and gave me the good news, I knew I had to act quickly before it was too late. I couldn't let her slip through my fingers again.

I must find a way to win her back over… to get her to trust and love me again. I know she thinks the father she once knew is gone, but she couldn't be more wrong. I am more than capable of being "dad", and the Malachi everyone fears. If Mya would just give me the chance to prove myself, I know she would be more than satisfied. I can give her any and everything her heart desires. Nice clothes, shoes, credit cards, laptops… you name it, and I can get it. Once she becomes settled with me, eventually, she would see my way as the right way… the only way. That being a Syphoner is the best way to live. Others will respect her, and she will become even more powerful; and who wouldn't want more power and respect? Eventually, she will learn to accept everything we do, and I do not want her to have to learn the hard way. Someone as influential as her can't be left in the wrong hands, I can help her grow to her full potential if she'll allow me. She doesn't know how special she is yet… she doesn't
~~~

understand that she is a Doppel Paladin and she can have the world in the palm of her hands if she chooses to. But if Mya decides to go against me… if she doesn't see it my way… if she's NOT willing to join me and my family syndicates… I can't bare the thought. I'd have to take from her what I deserve. As special as Mya is, I will not allow her to prevent my plans to take over every syndicate and overthrow the Elders who govern them. When I'm through, every person will know my name and fear me. She will learn that if she's not with me, she is my enemy!

Chapter 14

One month later

A car pulled up by the front entrance of school; Philip, my driver, hopped out of the front seat to open the rear door for me to get out.

"Thanks, Philip, " I say, getting out of the car.

"You're welcome, Ms. Yu. I'll be back to pick you up once school is over."

"Please call me Mya! And you don't have to come all the way back here to get me. I'm perfectly capable of getting home on my own."

"I'm sorry, Ms. Mya, but I have been given specific instructions by…"

"You have strict orders from my fa… Malachi," I let out a big sigh. "See you later, Philip."

I walked through the front doors, turned back and waved as I watched the car disappear around the corner. Sophia and Zohrah were sitting on the foyer bench, waiting for me. Excited to see my friends, I walked quickly towards them and pulled them into a group hug.

"How are you feeling?" I asked Zohrah. "You look well!"

"Thanks! I'm not 100%, but I'm getting stronger day by day," Zohrah replied with a smile.

"Are you going to The Underground tonight?" I whispered.

"Not tonight, probably tomorrow. I can't recover properly and train daily; training takes a serious toll on my body, so I go twice a week."

As we walked down the hall we pass Karina in conversation with a group of girls. She smiled slightly at Zohrah but realized she has no interest in being cordial. Karina bent her head in disappointment as any look of hope drained from her eyes. I thought of mentioning the idea of forgiving or, at the very least, hearing out Karina to Zohrah because I think it would benefit her if she could put it behind her. However, I know right now is not the right time, she's not ready.

We walked by all the cliques in the school, they all looked the same, but I felt different. I can't view anyone in the school the same after what I've witnessed and been through. How will I ever know someone isn't out to get me, or trying to get information from me to report to Malachi?

"You're right we do need to get better prepared. Do you mind if I come with you tomorrow?" Sophia asks Zohrah. "After what happened I could definitely use some training."

More students passed by, and we stopped speaking until they were out of ears reach.

"Hey… Mya, is it? I love your bag! It's a part of the new Hermes collection, right?" a girl from the pep squad clique gaped at my purse that swung on my arm.

"Uh… I guess so," I smile back. "It was a gift. I'm not really one to know all the new name-brand stuff," I said apologetically when I saw her face fall with disappointment at my lack of fashion knowledge.

"Well, whoever got that for you must love you because that bag cost more than many can afford. Surprised you even brought it to school… but like you said, you're not aware," she said, as she reached out to touch it but stopped herself. "Alright, I'll see you around, Mya."

She walked away giggling with her friends. I have no idea what I have in my closet, not since Malachi thought it necessary to upgrade my wardrobe. I protested for a while but gave in when my complaints went on deaf ears.

"Malachi gave you that bag, huh? And those new shoes, I presume?" Sophia asked, finally taking notice of my new items. "Interesting…"

"What's that mean?" I asked.

"He's obviously trying to buy your love," Sophia said matter of fact.

"You think so?" I say, feeling stupid for not thinking that before. "Maybe you're right. Should I not wear any of it then, you think?"

"Oh, please! Of course, wear it! As long as you are ahead of his game, you'll be fine. If you don't wear it, I sure as hell will," Sophia smiled. "Anyway, back to what we were talking about, which waasss… Z help me out here."

"We were talking about training…" Zohrah filled in.

"Right! Yes, you should come to Mya," Sophia suggested.

"I know, I know. I will, but not tomorrow night. I still have unfinished business to look into at home. I'm getting close I can feel it," I said.

"Still looking for the key?" Zohrah asked.

"Yep! I just know something isn't right… Malachi is hiding something and I intend on finding out what that is."

"Alright, well, let us know if you need anything… don't hesitate!" Sophia replies seriously.

"Don't worry, I will," I said as we reached my classroom door. "Hey Zohrah, how's Livia?" I ask hesitantly.

"She's alright for the most part, but she's worried about you, especially since you're living under the same roof as uuhhh…"

"You can say his name. Trust me no one is more irritated than me to find out who he really is."

My heart aches at the thought of Livia being worried, but I still feel hurt about her not telling me the full truth about Malachi.

"Tell Livia… I'll see her soon and not to worry. I know what I'm doing, and as soon as I know more, I'll fill you all in."

"By all, does that include Levi?"

Leave it to Sophia to bring him up at the most random times. I smiled slightly as my cheeks became warm. Butterflies skydive in my stomach at just the mention of his name.

"I'm actually seeing him tonight now that you mention it. So, yea, I'm sure he'd want to be filled in," I say, trying not to blush. "Anyway, class started, so I'll talk to you guys later."

I walked into Mr. Henry's class since last month he didn't bother pointing out when I got to class late. He doesn't bother me, and I do my best to pretend he doesn't exist. Once I finished with all my classes, I went outside and Philip was already waiting to take me home.

Since being forced to live with Malachi and Noreen, I barely leave my room; I only come out for food and when Noreen isn't around. It's still hard to be around her because I am still hurt by her betrayal. My stomach growled, so I went downstairs and made myself a sandwich. On my way back to my room, I heard the door to Noreen's room open; unable to think of an escape route, I realized I had no choice but to face her. As Noreen walked down the stairs and I went up, I passed her without looking at her.

"Aren't you tired of living like this? Noreen turned around and asked.

I turned back and looked at Noreen in her eyes, I thought of responding but decided it was best I didn't. Once in my room, I placed my plate down on the nightstand, reached for my TV remote and collapsed on my bed. Although I'm not fond of having to live here I have to admit my room is far better than I thought it would be. My walls are crisp white with large windows with curtains. My bathroom gives me the freedom to shower as long as I please. My king-size bed has more than enough space for me to roll around. My walk-in closet has far more space than any closet I've ever had. And my flat screen mounted on my bedroom wall and my PS5 (although I never play it) is just the icing on the cake. When I first arrived, my dresser had about 10 gift cards from different clothing stores for me to go shopping and a few electronics such as a phone and laptop. I gave the phone and laptop back to him immediately. I guess Malachi thought I needed an incentive not to run away the first chance I got. Sophia's words, "he's buying your love", rang in my mind. All the gifts made sense now, but I figured the best way to trick Malachi was to make him believe he was finally winning me over. Beat him at his own game. I couldn't help but wonder if Noreen got the same treatment. Taking a bite of my sandwich, my phone buzzed with a text message.

Levi: Hey, are we still on for later?
Mya: Yea... what time were you thinking of coming here?
Levi: Is 7 cool with you?
Mya: Sounds perfect!
Levi: Cool. I'll see you soon.

I checked the time to see how much time I had, it was 5 p.m. then, and Malachi usually gets home around 6ish every day. While exploring last week, I found a mysterious locked door behind a coat rack. I found it strange since Malachi showed me every inch of this house, or so I thought until I came across that door. I confronted him a few times about it, but my questions were swept under the rug. He expressed that it's an unfinished basement and no one ever goes down there. I realized I was never going to get the full truth from him, so I set out on a quest to retrieve the key so I could discover what was really in that basement for myself. I've searched high and low, which hasn't been easy with Noreen lounging around. However, yesterday, I made progress, I found a single key hidden in one of Malachi's drawers in a concealed compartment. I knew it wouldn't be a smart idea to take it at that moment, so I put it back and made sure his room was in the exact same condition as when I entered.

I tip-toed out of my room, and I could hear Noreen chatting away on her phone in her room. I couldn't wait any longer to see if the key I found prior would unlock the door to the basement. I walked slowly past Noreen's bedroom and entered Malachi's chamber. I quickly found the drawer with the hidden compartment and grabbed the key. I walked back down the hall, passing Noreen's room once again; I stopped by her door and pressed my ear against it. I heard the shower turn on in her bathroom as she started to sing along to Adele. I'd have at least 10 minutes to go downstairs, check the key in the door and place it back where I found it.

I sprinted down the stairs and onto the main floor. Although no one else was home besides Noreen, I stopped for a minute to check the hallway and ensure the coast was clear. I gently walked towards the mysterious door. I carefully placed the key into the lock and turned it; I held my breath until I heard the click.

I sighed with relief as I grabbed the doorknob and gave it a twist, shoving the creaky door open. I stood staring down the dark stairs leading to the basement and what potentially could be the answer to a lot of unanswered questions. Now that I knew for sure this key opened this door, all I needed to do now was somehow get a copy. I ran back to Malachi's room and put the key back. Everything in me wanted to go down and see what was in the basement, but once again, it was not the right time. Until then, my mission would have to wait.

Chapter 15

I had less than an hour before Levi would be outside waiting for me. I threw on jeans and a long sleeve shirt with clunky ankle boots and rushed downstairs as I received Levi's text message saying he would be there in 5 minutes. As I grabbed my keys from the hook by the front door, Malachi arrived, looking shocked to see me dressed to leave.

"Where are you off to?" he asked.

"Out," I answered curtly.

Although living here hasn't been as bad as I thought, I still couldn't forget how I got here and why I'm here. Malachi says, '*he wants to be a family, but I'm not sure he remembers how a family really works or, most of all… how a family treats each other.*' He can fill my closet with all the shoes, designer clothes in the world, it won't make me forget that he forced me to choose between living here with him or killing my friend.

"Mya…" he sighed. "When do you think you'll get past… everything that happened?" Malachi asked.

"Get past what exactly, you kidnapping me, Noreen drugging me or when one of your pets put a gun to my friend's head? Which part exactly do you want me to get over?"

"Forget I asked," he started to walk to the kitchen.

I stepped in front of him, blocking his path.

"No, listen! Buying me things won't make me love you. You need to prove to me that you are trying to be different. Show me you can change. I didn't ask to come here, so you can't expect this miraculous bond to happen overnight." I say, then move out of his way.

"I can't change you know that. I've invested too much already… I can't go back to how things were."

"Well ', *dad*' then you're wasting my time and yours. You might as well let me get back to my life."

"I can't do that either," he replied.

"Why not? Oh, right, you want things to be like when I was 11 years old again… you want me on your side," I chuckled. "Don't count on it."

Malachi gritted his teeth angrily, then closed his eyes and took in a deep breath.

"You'll change your mind… you'll see," he smiled. "Until then, we'll continue making up for lost time."

"Yea, right!" I replied as I rolled my eyes. "Don't wait up."

I smiled on the outside but I'm fuming within from her lack of appreciation for everything I've done for her. Does she not see I'm trying here? I didn't expect this to be an easy process, but… her attitude is relentless, and she's acting like a spoiled brat! She doesn't understand that I don't HAVE to treat her as nice as I have been… I could have her locked up … she has no idea the things I could do. I don't want to treat her like I do the others who refuse to abide by me. I need to remind myself that she's new to our world… she doesn't know how it feels to have matchless power at her reach. I love Mya, and I won't give up on her. As the saying goes… kill them with kindness. But if that doesn't work, I'll drop the kindness bit, and I'll do what needs to be done.

I slammed the front door angrily and quickly walked towards Levi, who was already waiting for me in the driveway. I was so livid I didn't even notice how amazing Levi looked. As I walked by him, he grabbed my arm, faced me and looked into my eyes.

"What's wrong?" he asked concerned.

"I don't want to ruin our evening with my issues," I said as he led me to the passenger door.

"Don't worry about all that… I'll drive, and you talk."

He kissed me on the forehead, and I felt my anger slowly start to disintegrate. Levi reversed out of my driveway, and I watched as the house got smaller in the review mirror.

"How do you like your new home?" Levi asked.

"You mean living with my abductor and manipulative sister?" I replied sarcastically. "How do you think I like it?"

"That good, huh?" he chuckled. "It's interesting because being close to your house, I can almost feel power radiating from inside."

"Well, Malachi is very powerful. We all know that already," I said, turning in her seat to face Levi.

"This feels different than what I felt in the alleyway that day."

"How so?" I asked.

"That day, Malachi felt powerful, but what I felt back at your place was like it was coming from dozens of people," Levi said.

"That's impossible. There are just three of us in the house."

"Well, Malachi has either gotten more powerful, or there are other people living in your house that you're not aware of."

I sat there thinking about what Levi said. Malachi does leave home on a daily basis, but where he goes is the real question. I'd hate to think that he's still prowling the streets stealing abilities from innocent people, but if he's addicted like he says, that's a high possibility. Is it likely for him to absorb that much power that it feels like it's coming from several people at once? How does he expect me to be an open book and allow him to fill that father role in my life when I have so many questions he refuses to answer?

"Earth to Mya," Levi says, touching my hand. "You zoned out for a bit… you good?"

"I'm fine. Great, actually" I smiled, pushing away those thoughts and deciding to focus on the present.

Hours later, Levi dropped me back home, and nothing could bring my mood down. I really enjoyed myself, and it was the first time in a few weeks that I didn't think or worry about this new world I'd been thrown into… I was able to finally live in the moment. Who knew mini-golf could be such a great distraction. As I walked through the front door, I saw Malachi sitting in the kitchen on a barstool. I pretended I didn't see him and quickly tried to rush up the stairs.

"Mya! Can you come here, please?" he called out.

"Yes?" I say as I reach the kitchen doorway.

Malachi grabs another stool and drags it beside him. I sit down.

"How was your date?" he asked.

"Is this what you called me here for?" I ask, getting up.

Malachi waved his finger, and my bottom was planted back on the stool.

"No, that's not why I asked you here," he continued. "I wanted to let you know that I'll be going away for a while."

"How long?" I asked.

"For about a week or so," he replied.

"Okay… are you going to tell me more, or is that it?"

"What more is there to tell you?" Malachi inquired, confused.

"How about where you're going and why?"

"I can't tell you that, but I'll be sure to check in with you and Noreen while I'm gone," he answered bluntly.

"Great… can I go now?"

Malachi sat quietly; I could see by the look on his face he wasn't finished with me.

"Soooo… that guy that picked you up tonight, is he your boyfriend?"

"Really! We're back to this?" I groaned, rolling my eyes. "Listen, if you can't answer at least one of my questions, I'm not answering yours."

I hop off the stool and start to walk out of the kitchen.

"Ok, wait! Ask me a question, and I'll answer; then I'll get to ask you," Malachi suggested.

"Where are you going?" I asked, turning back around and sitting down.

"New York, My turn; was that guy your boyfriend?"

"Nope," I replied. "Why are you going to New York?"

"Mya, you know I can't answer that."

"Then I guess we're done here," I shrugged. "I'm going to bed."

I sat for a moment and hoped he would object and tell me more. I hate to admit it, but I actually enjoyed this conversation. I wish I could see this side of him more often. Once I realized he wasn't going to budge, I said goodnight and went up to my room.

It's been a while since I've had to actually care for someone other than myself... well and Noreen. But Mya is different... she's always been different. Not an easy nut to crack. I realized after she left that I'm going to have to be more patient and understanding if I wanted things to go as planned. I'm going to have to remind myself how I was with her before all this blew up in my face. Be the daddy she remembers... then I think she will be more swayed to see things my way,

Everything will be all right, honey. Just calm down and breathe. I could feel the heat from the flames as they danced across

the town. The more my mother, Livia, spoke to me, the more at ease I felt. Eventually, the fire died down, and black smoke filled the sky. Livia held my hand as she led me away from the city. I looked back over my shoulder, and in the distance, I saw Malachi standing with Karina and Noreen. For the first time, I could see the hurt in his eyes as he stared at me, walking away.

"Mommy, I don't want to see the elders. Can't we just go instead? I swear I won't tell anyone what I did!" I plead.

"This is what's best, Mya. Now let's go."

I woke up and quickly wrote down what I remembered. Since finding out that my dreams are memories trying to resurface, I've been doing my best to piece things together. I got up and opened my bedroom door, and the smell of pancakes filled my room. It smelled so delicious; I can't remember the last time I had breakfast that didn't involve a bowl and a spoon. I went downstairs, and there was a full breakfast waiting on the counter, along with a written note from Malachi.

Girls,

I had to leave early. Please help yourselves to breakfast. I'll call you as soon as I can. Stay out of trouble, please. See you next week. Love you!

Dad

The house felt strangely empty without him there. I shouldn't care that he's gone; in fact, I should be happy and focused on the task at hand. With him being gone for a few days, I could finally get a copy of the key and see what he'd been hiding in the basement. But first, I'll eat… who can resist fresh pancakes?

After I ate, I decided to get myself together to start my day. I walked into my bathroom and grabbed my toothbrush and toothpaste when I heard Noreen turning on her bathtub faucet. I usually hear every conversation and note sung from her room since our spaces are parallel to each other. I realized this might be my only chance to swipe the key from Malachi's possession. I spat into the sink; I ran out of my room and went straight into the master suite. I ensured his door was closed behind me before I darted for the drawer where I last left the key. Sure enough, it was right where I left it; I grabbed it and carefully placed everything back as they were. I planned on cutting the key today, so…

In my peripheral vision, I saw a shadow of someone standing outside Malachi's door. The knob started to wiggle and turn as my stomach plummeted to my toes. Do I hide? There's no time! I quickly bent down and slipped the key into my sock just as the door swung open, and Malachi stood under the frame.

"HEEEYYY!" I sing, sounding overly excited and, I'm sure, very suspicious.

"Uh, hi… what are you doing in here?" Malachi asked as he stepped towards a bag on the floor that he must have forgotten.

"Well…" Think fast, Mya! "Well … I … I've never really seen your room, and I wasn't sure if you had left already, so I was coming to check, but… you were gone."

"Right. Didn't you see my note?" Malachi replied, unsure.

Crap the note!

"Right! The note! Yes, I saw it…I guess… I was just hoping you would still be here," I replied, praying he believed my story.

"Is this a long-winded way of saying you missed me?"

I could see a smile tugging at the corner of his mouth. I sigh with relief.

"Don't ruin it," I return the smile as we exited the primary bedroom.

The cool key slid deeper into my sock, and I shifted my weight onto my other leg. Malachi stopped me in front of my room.

"When I get back, how about we grab dinner? Or I can make your favourite dish…. You decide. Deal?"

"I never say no to good food," I laugh.

We stood awkwardly facing each other. I extend my arm for a handshake.

"Get back safe."

He takes my hand and pulls me in for a hug. My body stiffened immediately, but I forced myself to relax and enjoy his embrace.

"I'll see you soon," he says.

I hurried to my room as the feeling of guilt crept up on me for going behind his back and lying. I take my sock and shake it until the key falls into my hand.

I take one last glance around; both my daughters are in their rooms. I know she was searching for something, but the question is, what? I want to believe her, I still see Mya as the little girl I hurt so much all those years ago. Maybe she's coming around, and her explanation was the truth. Maybe she's finally beginning to view me as her dad. There's nothing I'd love more than to stay here and spend quality time with my girls, but I have business that needs to be dealt with elsewhere. I can't be Dad today I have to be Malachi.

He takes one last look around, then turns his gaze up to the ceiling where the outlining of the attic is. With a flick of one finger, the attic stairs ascended, and Malachi walked up and stopped in front of three wooden doors with different symbols engraved on the anterior of each along the back wall of the attic. He zipped up his sweater and pulled his hat low on his face. He opened one of the doors and stepped through.

Chapter 16

The Next Day

I took a shower, got dressed and went downstairs to prepare breakfast. When I arrived, Noreen was already in the kitchen looking through cupboards and the fridge. When we were on good terms, I was always the one who made the meals, and she tidied up. I walked by her, grabbed a bagel and some cream cheese, sliced my bagel and waited for it to toast.

"Where are you off to?" Noreen asked me trying desperately to make conversation.

I didn't respond, and I just stared at my reflection in the toaster.

"You have to speak to me sometime, Mya," Noreen huffed with her hands on her hips.

Still, I said nothing.

"I'm only asking because I have some errands to run, and Dad only left the one car for the both of us to share. We can ride together if you want," Noreen said while filling her mouth with a spoon of cereal.

She must think I was born yesterday to make such a statement. Ride? With her? HA! I thought of different scenarios for me to get what I needed to be done without anyone knowing. *I could get a ride from Phillip...*

but I don't want him to get any ideas. Levi is always working now. Since learning about Chuck's extracurricular activities with Malachi, he's been taking more shifts to keep a close eye on him. Well, I guess the bus is my only option.

"I'll take the bus," I finally say, biting into my bagel.

"Mya, don't be annoying! Just ride with me; you can't possibly hate me that much. It's not that serious," Noreen said, looking shocked that I answered her yet offended by what I said.

"Hate definitely isn't the right term," I reply.

"See, I knew you'd come around."

"More like… loath."

Noreen looked up, and I did my best to hold back my laughter; her reaction is priceless.

"You know what, Mya, you win. I tried. I thought it would be great to finally get past everything that's happened, but you're not willing to forgive. I'm done," Noreen said, throwing her hands in the air.

"Wow, Noreen, you really don't get it. You expect me to just turn around and forgive you for drugging me, lying to me, betraying my trust and not to mention smacking me over the head with a glass bottle with not even so much as an apology? I'm all about forgiveness, Nor but my issue is you don't even see what you did as wrong. I don't know how to turn the other cheek with you. I would have never in a million years done that to you! Ever! You meant way too much to me, and I considered you my family… my sister! Now, if you'll excuse me, I've lost my appetite," I said, fighting the tears that pricked my eyes.

I wrapped up the remaining of my bagel and left the kitchen.

"Wait!" Noreen calls out and follows me out of the foyer.

"What?" I turned and faced her.

"I'm sorry, okay. I never meant for things to go that far. Especially hitting you over the head and drugging you. You're just supposed to be so powerful that I didn't want to risk it."

"That's a terrible excuse."

"It is, but you have to understand; I've seen what you are capable of. I was there when the town went up in flames. Many people were injured because of you. Many people are scared of you, Mya, myself included," Noreen admitted. "I'm sorry, I went too far and I hope in time we will be able to move past this. Maybe friends again?"

I took a moment to truly listen to what Noreen said. Hearing her apology didn't exactly make me feel the way I thought it would. I thought instantly I would feel… closure or feel somehow better. But of course, nothing changed…I don't think I could ever forget what she did to me, but surely, I can forgive her…

right? She must have felt tugged between Malachi and I… tugged between what she had to do and what she wanted to do… but is that an excuse for her actions? I'm not usually one to hold a grudge… so I'll force myself to see past this. However, my guard will be up… my mind will be clear … and my eyes will be wide open this time around. There's no way I'd allow Noreen to trick me again… ever!

"Let's not get ahead of ourselves. We can start with I forgive you."

I cracked a smile finally, and I could see the pressure and guilt lift off Noreen's shoulders as she smiled happily.

"Yay! Awesome. So you'll ride with me then?"

"Are you crazy? I don't trust you!" I laughed hysterically. "But we can have an indoor movie night like old times if you want."

"That sounds perfect."

"I'll make my own drinks, though; I'm just saying."

"Whatever!"

I walked up a few more steps when I realized Noreen, and I had never had a chance to discuss what ability she acquired. Curiosity got the best of me.

"Hey, quick question," I said, turning back around.

"Yep?"

"Remember the time when you flung me into the wall like a rag doll?" I asked. "Is that your only ability, or do you have many like da… Malachi?" I inquired, hoping she didn't notice my slip-up.

"Oh, just the one," she replied. "Uh, why do you ask?"

"Just wondering if there's any more surprises I should be aware of. Alright, have fun running your errands," I said, continuing up the stairs.

The old me would have believed every word she said, but the new me knew better. And that right there was a lie.

I didn't want to have to lie to her again but what choice did I have? I don't want her to think I'm like our father because I'm not. I was forced to steal power from others to prove to him I was really on his side. I didn't enjoy it, and I'd rather never do it again. It's just when the pain from the addiction can consume you and take over your mind, body and soul. Before you know it, you're chasing someone and stripping them of their ability. And the thought of what I did to the love of my life all for a quick fix…poor Daniel. I couldn't even look at myself in the mirror, knowing what I'd done. She just forgave me, and I don't want to lose her again. I'd hide it for the rest of my life if I had to. One day, I'll stand up to Dad and tell him how I really feel. Hopefully, then this nightmare will end and I'll finally be able to forgive myself. I went into my room and locked the door behind me. I opened my bedroom window, sat on the ledge and swung my legs over onto the roof of our house. I looked around and nobody was around for miles. I took a step back, ran and jumped high into the air, landing on the roof of our neighbours. I sprung from house to house, loving every leap. I landed gracefully to make sure I didn't alarm those inside. What I was doing was risky, but this was the only time I truly felt free.

Chapter 17

Noreen

Past

Being an only child has its perks, but most times, I was extremely lonely. I used to ask my mom for a brother or sister but she always avoided the question. Thankfully, I had my best friend, Daniel, who lived across from me in our complex. It was a beautiful day as the sunshine peered through the drapes in my bedroom. It was summer so the temperature was warm from early morning. I got up, and around 11 am, I got dressed and went outside; Daniel was already waiting for me.

"Hey!" he said cheerfully as I stepped out of my door.

"Hey," I replied.

"What's wrong?" he asked, observing me.

"Promise you won't tell?"

"Who am I going to tell?"

"My dad was here last night… again. I just wish he could stay here with us… live here with us."

"Have you asked your mom about it?"

"Yes! All she says is that I won't understand. I've asked what she means by that so many times but all she says is she'll tell me when I'm older," I complained.

"That is weird."

"What should I do?"

"Don't worry, I'll help you come up with something," he smiles. "Come on, let's go find some other kids and play man hunt."

We ran around with the neighbourhood kids until my mother called me in for dinner. As usual, I asked if Daniel could stay and eat with us, and both of our parents agreed it was okay. Once the sun began to set. Daniel's mom called for him to come home.

"I'll walk out with you," I said, getting up.

I opened the front door to see people running in all directions. Daniel and I looked at each other, confused. My mom came running down the stairs as she heard the commotion from her room.

"What's going on there?" my mom asked rhetorically. "Come on, Daniel, I'll walk you home, Noreen. Please stay put."

I watched my mom guide Daniel through the sea of chaos. I stood there observing the crowd, wondering what the issue was. At that moment, I saw a young girl running in the street and a male, who looked a lot like my dad, chasing her. I noticed that as the girl ran, objects and people involuntarily moved out of her way, creating a clear path for her. Glass windows cracked as she sprinted by. The girl wiped her face on her sleeve, and she must have been crying.

"Mya! Mya let me explain. Stop!" Dad yelled.

Who's Mya, and why was she so upset?

"Dad? Dad!" I called out, but my calls went unnoticed.

I know my mom said to stay here for my own safety, but that's my dad out there. I have to make sure he's all right. He'll keep me safe once he sees me. I glanced at my mom, who was now speaking to Daniel's father. I take this chance to bolt and follow my dad; I dip and dodge people to keep up as much as possible. The wind howled and whipped around me, pushing me backward. The trees swayed, and dark clouds formed in the sky.

Distracted by all that was going on, I lost sight of my father. I followed a crowd that was headed outside my complex onto the road. Children screamed, looking for their parents. People were packing their vehicles with their families, trying to vacate the area. Who are they running from? I finally saw my dad still following the girl Mya; she scampered to the top of the hill that oversaw our city. Daddy stopped and turned back to look at his town and his people. He looked up at the dark sky and then back towards the scared citizens who were looking to him for guidance. I, too, was looking to him for answers.

"Dad!" I yelled again but he still didn't hear me.

Once Mya reached the top of the hill, she raised her arms up, and the winds became almost unbearable to withstand. I held onto a nearby tree to keep myself grounded. The trees bent, folding under the winds. The kids screamed and held on to each other, wanting it all to end. A man jumped into a vehicle and started driving away from the scene. Suddenly the man started fighting with the steering wheel like the car had a mind of its own. He made an abrupt sharp turn and hit a tree, knocking it down which then hit a power line. Screams arose as others started to notice Mya on the hill. Was she doing all this alone? Did she make that man hit the tree? The power line danced and landed on a car, sparking a fire which spread quickly. Within seconds, the fire was on the trees, on the roofs of houses, and on the lawns. The flames were everywhere, making it difficult to get away… the fumes began to choke me and burn my eyes. I watched as Mya stood on the hill observing what she'd done. Daniel ran up behind me.

"You have to get out of here! Your mom is looking for you!" he yelled with urgency.

"What are you doing here, Daniel? It's not safe."

"Come on, Noreen, we have to go!" he said, pulling my arm.

Just then, a large tree branch flew our way, whipping Daniel on his face. He yelled out in pain as he held his cheek; blood seeped through his fingers.

"Are you okay?" I asked, trying to see the wound. Just then, I saw my father helping people get away from the heat and smoke.

"There's my dad!" I pointed. "He'll keep us safe and get you cleaned up," I take off running.

"Noreen, wait!" Daniel bellowed, then followed.

"Dad! DAD!" I shouted, ducking from the flames and covering my nose from the smoke as I ran.

"Sweetie, what are you doing here? Where's your mom?" he asked, looking at Daniel and I. "What happened to your face, Daniel?"

"A tree branch hit me," Daniel said, still holding his cheek.

"Come on, you two, let's get you somewhere safe," my dad said.

He pulled us into his jacket, barring us from the smoke. My dad glimpsed up at Mya once more, and sadness filled his eyes; I sensed he didn't want to leave her behind. I tugged him along and turned back to Mya and saw a lady crouched down next to her. She was saying something to her, but whatever she said worked. The flames immediately subsided, and the dark clouds disintegrated. Everyone looked around for their loved ones to make sure they were unharmed. A few people were injured, but nothing severe. A few folks looked up and pointed at Mya as they murmured; some looked up at her in fear… others wanted her to pay for what she'd done.

"She's just a child," Dad pleaded with the town folk. "She didn't know what she was doing… sh…she couldn't control herself. Please… please don't place blame on her. She's just a child."

Some people nodded, understanding it could happen to anyone, losing control, especially being so young, while others simply walked away. A woman with short, dark, curly hair stared at my father with disgust in her eyes.

"Malachi, how can we take your word when you are not the same man we elected all those years ago? Huh? It's *YOU* who is to blame, not that child."

"Mrs. Medina, that is NOT…" he asked, looking perplexed.

"You think everything you've been doing is a secret?" she said, not letting him finish. "I know what you've been up to, and I can't wait until EVERYONE sees you for the scam artist you really are," she spat quietly. "Your reign over us won't last forever, Malachi… soon you will be nothing but a distant memory, and I can't wait until that day comes."

"Mrs. Medina, you are terribly mistaken," Malachi said, trying to remain calm.

"Malachi, please don't insult me by lying. Did you forget my ability is to detect when people aren't telling the truth? So please don't embarrass yourself," she smiled.

My father stood there with his body tense and his head low, thinking about what was just said to him. That was the first time I saw a change in him, and there was something different in his eyes. The hope and happiness I once saw were diminished. I glanced back one last time and Mya had vanished.

"Hey… hey, you there…what's your name?" Malachi asked a stranger walking by.

"Ian… Ian Henry," he replied.

"Perfect, Ian. Can you help me get these people away from here? Kids say hello to Mr. Henry."

"Hello, Mr. Henry," Daniel and I said in unison.

8 Years After the Fire

Daniel and I lay on the couch reminiscing about our childhood and how much things have changed in our world and between us.

"I can't believe it's been eight years since that day, and to think that girl... Mya can be out there somewhere," Daniel said.

"I know," I say, lying down on his chest and listening to the thumping of his heart. "But my dad will find her, I'm sure of it," I trace my fingertips along the scar on his cheek.

"There's so many Mya's in the world, though. Tracking her can't be easy," Daniel replied.

"True... but this is Malachi we're talking about... he always finds a way."

Daniel moved from underneath me and sat up, looking unsettled.

"What's wrong?" I asked, already sensing the issue.

"How are you so comfortable with what he's doing? Don't you want him to stop?" he inquired.

"Of course, I do! But what am I supposed to do? He's still my dad."

"I understand that, but wrong is wrong, babe," he says, shaking his head. "And I get the feeling there's something you're not telling me."

"What! NEVER!" I reply doing my best to sound sincere. "You know everything, I promise."

He pulled me in for a hug, and my throat tightened up as the hunger for power... the hunger to steal abilities from others nearly devoured me. My imagination started to run wild as I saw myself holding Daniel up by his neck while his power poured into me like a waterfall, quenching my thirst.

"Hey, Noreen!"

"Huh?"

"You were gone there for a second," Daniel said, rubbing my back.

"Oh… sorry just uh… I'm tired, I guess."

"Alright, I'll take you home soon. But first…" he said, presenting a flower pot filled with dirt.

"What's this?"

Daniel hovered his hand over the soil, and I sat staring, not moving a muscle. Slowly, the earth started to shift as a small green stem rose. It grew budding leaves thorns, and lastly, a red rose bloomed, standing tall. I smiled gleefully.

"You've been practicing," I giggle.

"Yes, I have," he smiled. "Happy one-year anniversary, babe."

"Thank you, Daniel. I love it… I love you!" I said, wrapping my arms around him for a warm embrace.

My throat stung as this repugnant addiction I faced tried to resurface once again. My body stiffened as my spirit fought the urge to do what my flesh felt was natural. Daniel kissed me, and I couldn't hold back any longer. I straddled him to the couch. Daniel welcomed me, trusting me, which excited me even more. I held his neck and leaned in, opening my mouth. At first, Daniel stared, unsure of what was going on; slowly, the horror set in, but by that time, it was too late. I inhaled in every inch of his ability, his identity, of *him!* I savoured every moment of it. I watched as the crow's feet around his eyes started to form. His dark hair lost its natural colour and became grey. His body shrunk beneath me. When I'm satisfied, I stand up and look down at Daniel and I …

What have I done? Wh… What have I DONE? I swore to myself I would never lose control with him. He was my safe haven, and this nauseating habit ruined it, ruined me! Daniel slowly turned and stared at me with disgust and hurt written all over his face.

"You're JUST like him! Actually, you are worse than him because at least Malachi is true to the monster he is," he spat. "You're a liar! You keep your abnormality locked inside until it can no longer be contained. You… are the worst kind of… evil."

And with that, he fainted. I stood shaking on the inside, he was right. No matter how much I tried to avoid it, this is who I've become. I need to get Daniel better and get him to forgive me. Show him I can change. I reach for my phone and dial.

"Hi, Dad. I need your help. I made a huge mistake."

I place my phone back in my pocket and then race to the bathroom, covering my mouth. I heaved over the toilet bowl until there was nothing left in me.

Chapter 18

As I entered my room, I grabbed my laptop, took a seat in my armchair and did a search for locksmiths in my area. Luckily, I found one a few blocks away from where we lived. I wrote down the directions and set out for the hike.

The sunshine beamed down on me as I walked, but the cool autumn breeze left a chill in the air. I strolled down each street, observing the scenery, I haven't done much exploring since moving to the suburbs. It's definitely a nice area and a step up from where we were in the downtown core. I saw children playing in parks, people walking their dogs and couples holding hands as they strolled along the sidewalk. When I arrived at the locksmith, no one was there, so I didn't have to wait too long before I had two keys, one in each hand. I made sure to pay cash so nothing could be led back to me. I quickly walked back home; I noticed the car was still in the driveway. Is Noreen still home? I searched every room in the house but no sign of her. Maybe she got a ride with someone instead. I need to make sure Noreen isn't planning on returning any time soon so I reached for my cell in my back pocket and dialled her number.

"Yes?" Noreen answers on the second ring.

"Hey, I was wondering that since you're already out did you want to pick up the usual snacks for movie night?" I ask, hoping she won't pick up on what I really want to know.

"I never say no to wine and popcorn. I'm on it."

"Perfect. Text me when you're close, and I'll meet you outside to help with the bags. Hey, I noticed you didn't end up driving; what happened?"

"Uh, oh yea, I got a lift from a uh friend of mine… Anyways, it'll be a while before I'm back, I have lots to do still, so I'll be about 2 hours. See you then, sis."

"Noreen?"

"Yea?"

"Don't do that."

"Ugh! Bye, Mya!"

Knowing I had more than enough time to spare and an empty house, I knew this was the best time to find the answers to the questions Malachi had been avoiding. I jet upstairs to Malachi's room and carefully placed his key back where I found it originally. I ran back downstairs, moved the coat rack to the side and stood in front of the door leading to the basement. I took the key out from my front pocket, pushed it into the lock, and turned gently. The door clicked when opened, which echoed through out the house. I placed my clammy hand around the doorknob and pulled the door open; the door creaked in need of oil. I opened the door just enough to slip inside then I closed it behind me. I rubbed my hands along the smooth wall, feeling for the light switch but none was found. I reached for the railing and used it to guide me down the stairs in the pitch dark; I could hear my heart pounding in my ears. I took my phone out and used the flashlight to see in front of me. At the bottom of the stairs, I used the light to look around me. For a basement that no one ever goes down there seems to be a lot of clothes lying around. A pungent scent hits me, and if this basement is off-limits, there shouldn't be a smell at all. I took a step forward, and I felt something graze my forehead and nose. I slapped my face and stifled a scream, thinking it was an insect of some sort; it was a string hanging from a ceiling bulb. I reached up and pulled the string; the basement lit up, and what I saw changed my life from that moment on. There were dozens of people crammed together. Some were standing, others were sleeping on cots on the floor, and some huddled in groups, whispering amongst each other. Men, women and teenagers were there, it looked like they were being held hostage, but why? As I stood there slowly, every one of them looked over at me, most looked like they recognized me, and they smiled with relief. Others stared at me nervously, unsure of my motives. I couldn't help but wonder if everyone here knew of the fire I started years ago, I wondered if they were scared of me like Noreen said. As I got closer, I noticed the people lying on cots look frail and elderly.

Right away, I remember Zohrah lying on a cot in the underground looking just like this week's prior. Is that what happened to them? Were they striped of their power as well? So many thoughts were racing through my mind, but Levi's words finally made sense. He was sensing all these people down here; he was feeling their power. Part of me wanted to turn around and run up those stairs and forget what I saw here today, but that's impossible there's no going back now. I looked closer and noticed every person down there had chains around their ankles, and this proved they were being kept here against their will. My heart filled with sadness and anger. If Malachi did this he must be stopped.

I heard chains dragging against the cement floor, I looked in the direction the sound was coming from and as a man shuffles over to me. He looked like he'd been here a long time, ragged and unshaven. His clothes were tattered and dirty, and his skin looked like it hadn't seen the sun in a decade. Yet something about him felt familiar, and there was something in his eyes that made me think I knew him or should know him. He continued to stare at me, and I him.

"Mya?" the man finally asked.

"Yes? Who are you?" I asked, squinting.

"My, you've grown up to be a beautiful young lady. You resemble your mother tremendously. Of course, you wouldn't remember me, and it's been so long since we've seen each other."

I kept staring at him because deep down, I knew he was right. In my heart, I knew I'd met this man before.

"My name is Michael. I'm your…"

Streams of memories played in my mind like a slideshow. I saw his face, heard his warm voice, and recalled the fun moments we had together. How could I have forgotten the man who helped me through it all? The one who was there when Malachi was too busy nursing his dirty habit.

"Uncle Mike?"

Chapter 19

Michael part 1

21 Years ago

I needed to see the world for myself. I've heard many rumours and stories about humans and their lack of acceptance for others who are different. But I wanted to form my own opinion, and of course, I wasn't going to be foolish and show anyone my gift. I love my city and people, but I'm mentally drained from being the Elder's constant eyes and ears of the community. They trusted me, which I knew in the long run would be a great asset if I ever needed a favour. The only down fall is the Elders always wiped my memory after every visit, and the recovery was starting to become more difficult week after week.

By my 20th birthday I saved up enough to venture out on my own. My parents weren't too thrilled with the idea, and by parents, I really mean my mother. My brother on the other hand, Malachi, didn't seem to mind the idea and was very supportive.

"Do what you need to do for yourself," he advised.

"Thanks… it's not forever… I just need time to … you know… figure things out and be on my own," I explained.

The next day, I left our secluded world and didn't look back. I traveled for a year, saw many different cultures and people and learned a few languages. Everyone seemed to accept me with open arms. Nobody knew my secret but I began to wonder whether the things I was told about the humans were true. Yes, some could be judgemental, but there were people who I knew accepted others for who they were. They didn't care about how different others were and I knew if they had an inkling about my supernatural abilities, they wouldn't. I realized that having abilities doesn't make you different unless you choose to let them become who you are. Inside, we are all the same, and we are all equal.

One night, my Nokia cellphone buzzed with a message from Malachi.

Malachi: I'm getting married, and you're my best man. Get your butt home.

I packed my bags and was back home the next evening. It felt surreal to be back home, in my bed, but I was too exhausted thinking about it.

The next morning, I woke up to my mother sitting at the edge of my bed, beaming down at me.

"Ma! Are you serious?" I rubbed my eyes.

"My sweet boy is home, let me see your face," she grabbed my cheeks.

"C'mon… how about I'll get up in an hour and help with breakfast?" I asked, hoping she would leave.

"Breakfast is almost done. Be down in ten minutes… you hear me?"

"Mmmm," I mumbled.

"Michael!! Ten minutes!" she demanded.

"Okay, ma, ten minutes, I got it."

There was no point in arguing. I swung my legs over the bed and sat up. I stepped into some shorts, not bothering with a shirt. I used the bathroom and got downstairs with three minutes to spare. Still tired, I lay my head on the dinning table and closed my eyes. I heard footsteps behind me.

"Do you need my help to set the ta…"

As I stood up to offer my mother a hand with what ever she needed, I saw a vision of beauty. This woman was a sight for sore eyes; she's possibly the most gorgeous woman I've ever seen.

"Uh… you're not my mom," I finally said.

"No, I most certainly am not," she laughed, showing her immaculate smile. Is that a dimple on her cheek? We stared at each other for what seemed like forever.

"So, are you friends with the family orrr? You know my mom, I presume," I say, motioning for her to sit down.

"Mmm, you can say that. You're Michael, right? I've heard so much about you."

"Good things, I hope, and you are?" I asked, reaching for her hand.

"Livia," she replied, placing her hand in mine.

I kissed the back of her hand, and from what I saw, she blushed. *Pace yourself, Michael,* I thought to myself.

"Pleasure to meet you, Liv, may I call you that?" I asked, returning a smile.

"Sure," she said, releasing her grip and taking her hand back.

"I have to be honest," I leaned in to whisper. "You have to be one of the most be…"

"Is that who I think it is?" Malachi's voice boomed, interrupting me. He greets me with a huge hug. "Glad you're back, brother, I've missed you."

"I've missed you too… looks like you've gained a few," I said, slapping his stomach.

He pushed me playfully.

"Boys, stop the silliness and let's eat," Mom says, coming down the stairs. "They've always been like this," she smirked, nudging Livia.

My eyes locked with Livia's once more, and she smiled. I felt an instant connection with her. There's something about her that's gravitating; I need to know more about this woman.

"So, I see you've met the future Mrs.," Malachi said, disturbing my fantasy.

"Huh," I replied, not paying attention.

Malachi walks up to Livia and pulls her in for a longing kiss. That caught my attention.

"Michael, I'd like you to meet Livia. My fiancé," Malachi radiated with happiness and love.

"Oh… man… wow, congratulations, man," I replied, pulling them both in for a hug.

My eyes glanced towards her left hand, which bore no ring.

"She's getting it resized," Malachi said, following my gaze.

"I'm really happy for you, man; you deserve it."

"Thanks, Mike. I appreciate that."

Mom brought breakfast to the table and we all devoured everything within minutes. As soon as I was done, I excused myself and went straight to my room to attempt and erase any feelings I had towards Livia. I needed to put my emotions in check.

4 months later

"To Malachi and Livia!" I said, raising my glass of champagne.

The crowd cheered, lifting their glasses, and clapped as the happy couple kissed. They picked the perfect day for their wedding. I don't recall ever seeing my brother look this happy. I watched Malachi as he led his new wife to the dance floor, spun her around then pulled her in close as she threw her head back laughing. I took a look around as other couples joined them, swaying to Luther Vandross. Caterers passed by offering delicious h'orderves; I grabbed a few off a platter. I loosen my tie; my best man duties are officially over. I sit down at an empty table, eating my handful of appetizers as I watch Malachi dance with his beautiful bride.

"They look so happy, don't they," mom said from behind me.

"Yea, they do," I observed.

She pulled up a chair and sat beside me; we enjoyed the scenery for a few moments.

"How long do you think it will be until you're over this crush?" She asked nonchalantly.

"Ma, what are you ta…"

"Don't play dumb with me, son. I know you! Besides, the long stares when she's not looking gave you away."

"It's nothing! She's pretty, that's all," I rationalize. "It was over months ago. He's my brother I'd never hurt him like that."

"Mmm, maybe not intentionally, but history has proven that one thing can drive a wedge between family, especially men, is a woman. Make sure that never happens."

"Ma, you're over-exaggerating," I joke. She looked at me, and I stopped laughing once I realized how serious this was to her. "It won't happen; you have my word," I leaned in and gave her a peck on the cheek.

"It better not," she smiles, taking my face in her hands. "There are plenty of beautiful women here. Ask one to dance."

"Alright, you've made your point."

"Good! I'm going to find your father."

I watched my mother get lost in the crowd. She was right, and I had to move on from this... what ever this is. I stood up, and I noticed a girl standing by the bar by herself, watching the other couples dance. She had on a stunning navy-blue dress that showed off her figure. I looked back at my brother and Liv, whatever I thought I felt between us, I couldn't have been more wrong. This ended now. I inhaled and walked away from my past and toward my possible future.

My husband held me close as we move to the music on the dance floor. We laughed; he whispered the sweetest things to me. He always knew just what to say to make me feel like I'm the most beautiful woman in the room. He was such a gentle, kind and loving man, more than I've ever experienced from anyone before, which was why the guilt was eating away at me. I looked beyond this perfect man and see Michael. The man I was attracted to the moment I set eyes on him in the kitchen some months ago. I should have told him right there and then who I was, but… at that moment, I wasn't ready to face my truth. I was already committed to one man, yet my heart yearned for another.

Chapter 20

Michael part 2

1 year later

I always hated the scent of hospitals but this floor was different. Doctors walked frantically from room to room with nurses trailing behind. The hallway echoed with groans from women in pain, but then the beautiful cries of a new born baby filled the air, making everyone around who heard stop and smile.

"Michael?"

I turned to see Malachi cradling a precious human being in his arms so delicate and small.

"I'd like you to meet your niece, Mya," Malachi says, placing her in my arms.

"She's precious, man," I say, staring down at her in awe. "Just beautiful."

"Yes, she is," Malachi smiles back. "I have something else I want to share too."

"What?"

"The votes are in…" Malachi says, barely able to contain himself.

"And?" I asked, looking up at him excitedly.

"The people have elected Liv and myself to run the colony," he said proudly.

"That is amazing news! We have two things to celebrate now," I say, bringing my attention back to Mya.

"There's more," Malachi continues. "I want you to be my right-hand man."

"Mmm… I don't know if that's the best idea, man. You know that's not really my thing."

"I know Michael, but think about it," he said, sitting beside me so others couldn't hear. "Between your gift of seeing, my gift of strength and Livia's gift of inflicting and manipulating emotions, we would make the perfect team. Not to mention, you are allies with the Elders; they trust you. Just say you'll at least think about it," he pleaded.

"I'll think about it," I sighed.

"Thanks, bro… that's all I ask," Malachi said, reaching back for Mya. "Thanks for coming, call me tomorrow so we can discuss more ideas I have."

"Alright, I will," I said, standing up to leave. "Hey… uh, how's Liv doing?"

"She's awesome, man, a real fighter. You want to come say hi?"

"Nah… tell her hello for me."

"You sure? I'm sure she wouldn't mind you popping your head in," Malachi tried to convince me. "Believe me, I'm sure. Go back to your wife, I'll talk to you later."

Since having that talk with my mother, I've made sure to steer clear of Livia until I know for sure I'm over her. And if I have to be around her for family events, I'd make sure to keep my eyes on the ground so her simplicity doesn't mesmerize me. I have yet to encounter another woman who has the capability to hold my attention like Liv can. I won't stop believing my future wife is out there waiting for me; surely, I can't go on for the rest of my life lusting after my brother's wife. That's something that would weigh too heavy on my heart.

While I drove home, I weighed my pros and cons of working with Malachi. The commitment I had with the Elders kept me busy enough as it was. But I knew it would be a huge asset for both my brother and The Elders if I worked with Malachi. For sure, The Elders would want to know my brother's plans for the city, and me having their trust will definitely come in handy for if and when I needed a favour. I'd be foolish not to take this opportunity whether I wanted to or not. Sometimes, you have to set aside what you want for the betterment of your community and family. I guess my decision has been made.

Mya's 5ᵗʰ birthday

"Happy birthday, baby girl," I said as I handed her a big wrapped box.

"I'm not a baby, Uncle Mike," she replied, giggling.

"Of course, you're not… but you're still *my* baby girl. Is that okay with you?" I asked.

"Hmmm," she rubbed her chin as she contemplated. "Okay! You can call me that. Can I open my present now?" she asked excitedly.

"Yes, you may," I sat back and watched her tear the paper to shreds.

"Hey, Michael… can we talk?" Malachi came up from behind and tapped me, looking uneasy.

"Sure, what's up?" I asked, finally taking a proper look at my brother.

"Not here… let's go out back."

He didn't seem like his usual self. The bags under his eyes indicated lack of sleep, he paced back and forth, signifying something important was on his mind. I knew since taking on the role as a leader in our town a few years ago he has been extremely overwhelmed. Being a new father and thrown into a new career practically on the same day can take a toll on anyone. We walked to the backyard where no one could overhear us. Malachi fidgeted and opened his mouth to speak but closed it again.

"What is with you, dude?" I asked, trying to be patient.

"I have something to tell you… I've wanted to tell you this for a long time."

"Alright, I'm listening."

"Well… there's this woman…"

"Wait… wait! Please tell me you are not about to say what I'm thinking," I groaned as I rubbed my temples with my fingertips.

"Listen, it was *ONE* time! And it's never happening again," he explained, trying to justify his own actions.

"Wow, man… I can't believe what I'm hearing. So tell me something… why are you out here telling me and not your wife?" I yelled.

Malachi reached into his pants pocket, pulled out a small wallet-size photo and handed it to me. I looked down at the picture and saw an adorable little girl with curly red hair smiling at the camera.

"Cute kid. Who is she?" I asked.

"Her name is Noreen… she's my daughter. I need you to cover for me."

"Your daughter! How could you do this to your family man?" I asked as I thought how much this would break his family's heart. "And how the hell do I cover for you?"

"I haven't exactly had time to see Noreen, and her mother said I could only see her today," Malachi said desperately.

"So, the only day and time you can see Noreen is during Mya's birthday party? Does Noreen's mother know about your family? Wait, how can she not? Everybody knows who you are… you're high profile." I said in disbelief of what I was hearing.

Malachi hung his head like a young child being reprimanded.

"You think this is how I wanted things to turn out, Michael? But what am I supposed to do? I can't just abandon Noreen when I know she's my daughter. I just need time to figure this whole thing out… and time to figure *out how I'm going to tell Liv the truth," Malachi said,* sounding frustrated.

"I can't lie and say I understand where you're coming from because I don't. But… I'll cover for you but only for this one time. Where do I say you went?" I asked.

"I don't know, just figure it out!"

"Listen, when your *wife* asks where you disappeared to later, our stories need to align," I spat.

"Just text me whatever you tell her, and I'll keep the same story. Just do me this solid, please!" Malachi besought.

I stood there in silence, unsure how to respond. I understand he is my blood, but does that mean I aid him when he is doing something wrong as well?

"I understand I disappointed you, Michael, but I'm human. I made a mistake."

"Then tell her that," I responded, pointing back to the house.

"I will… eventually, just not today. You are my brother… you're supposed to have my back no matter what. Whose side are you on?"

"Oh, you want to pull that card?"

"It's not a card. It's reality, man. Now, are you going to help me or not?"

I stand face to face with Malachi for a moment, wondering if this newfound "fame" has gotten to his head this much that he thinks he could get away with this.

"It's gotten to your head, hasn't it," I smirk. "Being in charge has made you think that you are invincible. But you know what, go do what *you* have to do… I'll take care of *your* family."

Malachi stands back and examines me, staring like he is trying to solve an equation in his head.

"What?" I asked.

"I can't help but wonder why you're so interested in… actually, never mind. I'll be back, thanks."

I watched as my brother walked away. Why didn't I see this coming? I always make a conscious effort to block seeing my family to respect their privacy. Today, that has to change; I'll be keeping a close eye on Malachi from now on.

"Hey, Michael," Livia called out to me from the back door. "Have you seen Malachi? We're about to cut the cake."

"Oh… uh yea," I say, jogging back towards her. "He had to step away, you know… duty calls," I lied, hoping she didn't ask anything more than that.

"He promised no work today!" she sighed. "Should we wait? Do you know how long he will be?"

I hesitated for a minute.

"Don't wait, cut the cake."

6 years later

"Hey Michael, take a walk with me."

"Do I have a choice?"

"Nope. Let's go."

For the past several years, Malachi and I have had issues with our brotherhood. Our relationship has strained. I'm not sure how to fix it or if I want it fixed. Since finding out about this illegitimate child, he has shielded many other things from me. He's started hanging out with other people who seemed to be more of "yes men" than true friends. His position of being the head of our colony has made him think he is superior to the rest of us. We all still work together, and I am still doing my weekly duties for the Elders, but I've been contemplating going back out into the world to travel and clear my head. I've seen far too much of what Malachi has done lately and what he plans on doing that I'm not sure I can stand to watch him go down this spiral.

I followed Malachi to a private wooded area. The further we walked, the fewer people were around. Evergreen trees surrounded us, and the dirt path we followed soon faded away. My heart nearly burst through my chest in fear, but I made sure I kept my cool. I didn't want to give Malachi any indication that I knew what his plans were. And I did; I just knew the future always had a way of changing. I haven't told anyone what I've seen, especially not the Elders, which would be a huge violation if they found out. Finally, we stopped; two men were already there waiting for our arrival. We all faced each other and waited for someone to speak.

"Do you know why I brought you here, Michael?" Malachi asked.

"No idea," I lied.

"I know you have the ability to see… I want to know what have you seen."

"Nothing," I swallow. "Why?"

"I don't have time for your lies, Michael. Have you been spying on me? Be honest!" Malachi said calmly.

"Honestly, Malachi," I paused, "I don't have time for your games… is this why you summoned me here? To interrogate me when I've done nothing to you?"

Malachi marched up to me, grabbed me by my throat with one hand and lifted me into the air. I gasped for air while kicking my feet and trying to pry his fingers off my neck.

"Yes!" I finally let out. "I've looked."

"So, you know…?" Malachi asked.

"Yes," I wheezed. "You've been stripping people of their gifts."

Malachi released his grip, and I coughed uncontrollably.

"Who have you told? Have you told the Elders?" He questioned.

"Absolutely not! If I told them, do you think you'd be standing here right now? They would have taken you in already," I said, reminding him of the rules.

Malachi nodded in agreeance.

"What's going on with you, man? I'm your brother I have your back regardless, you know that. Talk to me!" I reasoned with Malachi.

"Michael, I have a proposition for you. I want you to embark on this journey with me."

"You are crazy," I choked on my laughter.

I tried to leave, but his friends blocked my path.

"Why not Michael? Think about it! You can become omnipotent. What person in their right mind wouldn't want that?"

"Well… me! Besides everyone already is starting to see a change in you since you've been elected. You went from a relaxed family man to God knows what in a span of a few…"

"Who's everyone, the feeble-ass Elders that are nearly knocking on heaven's door? Are they supposed to scare me? Or is it my dear wife, Liv? Has she been whispering how much of a horrible husband I am? Have you been imagining yourself as her prince charming coming to save her from the evil brother? For years, I've seen how you've looked at her… how you've avoided her!"

"Did you notice that before… or after you had Noreen?" I snapped glaring at Malachi, daring him to make his move.

We stood glaring at each other in silence.

"Join me," Malachi asked once more, clenching his fists at his side.

"Not a chance," I replied.

"Wrong answer."

Suddenly, Malachi grabbed my neck again and raised me into the air. I fought, kicked and tried to loosen his grip, but Malachi's strength couldn't be wavered. The sudden image that I saw earlier that day came back to my thoughts and I knew what was to come next. Malachi opened his mouth and started to inhale my ability. I could feel the agonizing pain from the depths of my soul where he stole my identity; our abilities were a part of us. My flesh began to shrink and wrinkle before my eyes; I could no longer fight to get away. Although I thought I was mentally prepared for this moment, I don't think I truly was ready to believe he would actually do it to his only brother. The pain continued to seep into every pore of my body. But just as I saw this happen in my vision, I knew there was more. I knew we were being watched… an innocent girl who watched intently as everything unfolded. Malachi stopped and dropped me, my bones brittle bones cracked as I hit the dirt. I lay groaning on the floor but waiting… waiting for the one word that would leave Malachi speechless.

"Daddy?"

Malachi chased Mya through the woods trying to explain, trying to undo what she saw. But it was too late. What she saw could never be undone.

In a few months, my ability was fully restored. Most times, I pretended that my gift hadn't been the same since that day which has kept Malachi off my back. I knew the only way I could stop Malachi would be to allow myself to be captured. To end up here in this basement for Mya to find me, find all of us. No matter how long it took, I had to keep faith that this basement was exactly where I was supposed to be.

Chapter 21

My eyes filled with tears as I looked at the man who used to give me piggyback rides, took me bike riding, took me to see all my favourite movies. And now, he looked powerless and vulnerable.

"So you do remember me?" he asked.

"Certain things have come back to me, yes," I answered.

"I see," Michael said, impressed.

We walked towards the back wall by a deserted cot; we sat down to continue our conversation.

"So," I said, looking around. "Why are you all here?"

"I think you already know the answer to that, Mya. The real question isn't why, it's how."

He was right. I just didn't want to admit to myself the truth about my father.

"Okay, so how did everyone get here?"

"Most of us were captured, others followed Malachi here."

"Why would anyone follow him?" I asked, confused.

"Your mother and father were very respected amongst our people. Some have a hard time believing that he is a bad man. We've all heard the rumours, but unless people saw it for themselves, they refused to believe. Many don't want to believe he's changed, so they allowed themselves to fall into his web of lies."

"Okay, but why do people care so much? He's only one man. It's one thing to be looked up to, however, it's another to be idolized," I replied.

He looked at me, confused; it became apparent there was more to the story I didn't know.

"Mya, your father is, or I should say was, the leader of our people. Both him and your mother."

"My parents were leaders? So, like king and queen? Prime Ministers? What do you mean?"

"They still lived amongst us, but they were elected by the town people to make important decisions when necessary. They were the voice for the people."

I took a moment to let that penetrate my thoughts. Another secret my mother had kept from me. I couldn't help but wonder how many more lies would be uncovered.

"Mya, you are the key to the survival of our people. You can put a stop to all of this madness."

"What... Me? HOW?"

"You are much more powerful than you realize, more powerful than anyone I've come in contact with. With practice and consistency, you will by far become the most influential person in our existence," Michael replied. "You're power right now is triggered by emotions, happiness, sadness but most of all anger."

"Just like when I set the town on fire because I couldn't control my anger," I recalled.

"That's right."

We sat for another moment.

"That's not all," Mike continued. "There's another reason you're special. You are what we call a Doppel Paladin."

"A Doppel what now?" I asked, looking horrified.

"Our people are born with one ability, but you were born with two."

"So I'm a Doppel Paladin, which means I possess two abilities? How is that even possible?" I asked.

"That's partly what it means. You are the only one that we've seen it happen to so far, that I know about anyway," he replies.

I sat silently; I was not sure how much more information I could take. I'd been Mya all my life, and now I was called a Doppel Paladin? What did that mean? This was difficult, but I needed to know more, I needed to push through.

"Wow! This is a lot," I said, exhaling. "How will I know what my other ability is?"

"Well the night the fire took place, you tapped into both. So much more happened that you don't remember. Eventually the memories will resurface, but you need to be prepared because you may not like what you see."

I nodded in agreeance.

"Once those memories return, I need you to remind yourself that you were just a young child when it happened. You had no control of what you were doing or your emotions. None of it is your fault; it's Malachi's carelessness and greed that brought all this on," he said.

With every word he spoke, his eyes darkened with anger and bitterness. Remembering I was on a time limit, I continued with my questions.

"I've seen older pictures of you and Malachi. How is it possible that Malachi looks exactly the same as he did all those years ago?" I asked curiously.

"Our people age slower than regular humans. Because Malachi strips the innocent of their power, he takes a bit of their youth along with it. In turn, he will stay younger even longer than he normally would."

"You keep saying our people… who are we? What are we?"

"When Malachi decided to go down the wrong path, we separated into three divisions, the Pacifists, Siphoners and the Agros. The people who follow Malachi are called the Siphoners."

"What is the difference between the three?"

"Siphoners will do anything for more power, they will strip abilities from whoever they get their hands on. Unfortunately, I've seen it happen before, and it literally looks like they are being sucked from their body and into the Siphoner through their mouth. It's the most tragic and violent thing I've ever witnessed," he said sorrowfully. "Pacifists are the peacemakers. They don't want anyone to get hurt. They just want things to go back to how it once was. The Agros are our warriors. They believe Malachi should perish for what he's done. They believe we should shoot first, no questions needed."

"I assume everyone here is a Pacifist?" I asked, looking around.

"That's right. Some are a bit more passive than others, but they just need a push or someone to show them the way," he said, looking straight into my eyes.

I knew why he was looking at me, but I quickly turned away.

"So let me just recap: I'm a Doppel Paladin, my father who is also the villain, was the leader of our people but is now the head of the Siphoners. My mother, who was also a leader, is a Pacifist, am I right? And then there's me, stuck in the middle. Is that all?" I asked.

"Don't forget you're the key," he smiled.

"Oh yes… how could I forget that," I replied. sarcastically

More silence followed.

"I know this is a lot to take in at one time," Uncle Mike said. "But I have a feeling you're a lot stronger than you realize. But please, Mya, if you have more questions, ask me while you can."

"Thank you for being honest, it feels like everyone in my life has lied to me," I replied. "But can I ask you a personal question?"

"Of course."

"How were *you* captured?" I asked hesitantly.

"I wasn't," he answered as a smile spread across his face.

"So you FOLLOWED him?"

"Malachi thinks he captured me, but I wanted to be caught. If he weren't so blind with power, he would have seen right through my charade," he said.

"Why are you here then?" I asked.

"I'm here for you, Mya."

"Me? Why me?"

"Like I said, you are the key. You are the one who will put a stop to all this chaos," Michael reminded her.

"Well how did you know I'd come, and how do you know I'm supposed to save everyone? How can you be so sure?"

"From when you were a child, you were very observant, curious and determined. I knew you'd find the door to this basement and I knew you wouldn't stop until you knew what was down here," he explained. "And how I know you are the one who stops my brother is because I can see it. I have the gift of seeing. Just like you have dreams or visions, mine happen in picture form. No sound, just images."

"Let me get this straight. You expect me to go against my father, the most powerful person of our people right now, and beat him by myself?" I asked.

"Of course not, you'll have help!"

I looked around the basement; *If these people are his idea of help, we might as well quit now,* I thought to myself. Michael followed my gaze.

"This isn't all of us; there are many more. There are a total of four camps across the globe. We all live amongst regular humans hiding in plain sight," Michael said. "The first group is here in Toronto."

"The Underground?"

"Majority do live in The Underground, but there are others hiding in plain sight," his eyes lit up excitedly. "The other camps are in China, Lebanon and New York. Pacifists and Agros are located at each place, but because both divisions disagree with their methods, they went their separate ways."

I sat up straight, hearing where the last location of where the groups were located.

"Malachi told me he was headed to New York for a few days. Do you think he's trying to find them?" I asked.

"That's a possibility."

My head felt like it was spinning. How was I supposed to be this saviour to these people when I was still trying to figure out who I was? I was not sure I could do this, but from the looks of it, I didn't have much of a choice.

"Somewhere in this house, there are portal doors that lead to each city where each camp resides," Michael continued.

"How will I know what these portal doors look like?" I asked.

"Each portal door has a symbol engraved on it."

"A symbol?" I asked, confused.

Michael takes his hand and pushes his sleeve up, revealing the same symbol tattoo Malachi has on his arm. I stare in astonishment.

"I've seen this on Malachi too," I finally said.

"When things were… how they were, each person received a symbol when their ability reached full maturity."

"And when does that happen?"

"On your 21st birthday," he replied

I just turned 20, I thought to myself.

Michael continued to speak, "Back then, these symbols represented each camp. But since Malachi started this mess, the symbols no longer appear."

I sat for a moment, taking in all the information I just heard.

"So what do I do once I enter these portals?"

"You must speak to the elders of each syndicate. Usually there are two Elders that signify each division. When they are on your side tell them you will give them word as to when everything will take place, tell them to prepare for the worst," he said.

"Who are these elders anyway? Why do I need to go to them?" I asked.

"Elders are the only people in each division who can erase memories. They have the absolute final say when it comes to each division and the policies," he explained. "The Elders were very angry with the path your father chose to pursue."

Immediately, I remembered Livia taking me to see the Elders in my dream and me pleading not to go.

"Is that where my mother took me after..." I felt sick to my stomach.

"Mya, your mother thought she was doing what was best for you," he tried to comfort me.

"Yes, but she could have told me when I saw her recently. She could have explained that SHE had my memories ERASED, and that's why I'm in this predicament now!" I exclaimed.

We sat in silence once more as I processed what I'd learned. How could my mother not tell me the whole truth?

"So if I go to these Elders and tell them what's going on... who's to say they'll even believe me?" I asked Uncle Michael.

"Tell them I sent you, and you won't have any problems."

"Ok no offense, but why would they care if you sent me? Why does your name hold any merit?"

He took a moment before he explained.

"Back then, your father and I were inseparable. I was his right-hand man. We made decisions together, he trusted my judgment, and along with my gift we were always able to make sure things stayed in order within the city. He would never admit it, but I was the brains behind the operation. Your father was more of the spokesperson; everyone loved him."

"That doesn't answer my question," I cut him off impatiently.

"I wasn't finished. The Elders often summoned me because of my gift of seeing. They would ask me what I saw and trust that I would tell them the truth, which, of course, I always did. Once I was done, they would wipe my memory so I wouldn't have to bear the burden of knowing everything they did."

"Orrr, they didn't trust you, and they thought you would betray them," I retorted.

"That's exactly what your father thought for a long time. He wasn't a fan of the Elders using me for my gift."

"Did it bother you?"

"Whether I liked it or not wasn't my concern; it gave me a name with the Elders. They respected me because of my cooperation. And because I never complained or objected, they learned to trust me."

"You must have seen what Malachi was planning before anyone knew though, right?"

There was silence.

I sat there going over everything in my head. Uncle Mike kept referring to me as "the key", but how could he be so sure? He had the gift of seeing, but it didn't make him all-knowing. And how could I go against Malachi and his people, who were bigger and way more advanced than I was? But the one thing that stuck out in my mind the most was, what if I could change Malachi…?

"I don't think I can do this," I said, holding my face in my hands.

"Okay… why not?"

"Look around, Uncle Mike. This is too much. I don't want to turn my life upside down for people I don't even know or remember."

"Weeks ago you didn't even know our world existed or about your gifts. Your life will change whether you want it to or not. You're scared, and I understand that, but it seems to me that you're looking at how big the problem is and not trying to see the positive outcome that could take place."

"Of course I'm only seeing the problem. I'm not the one with the gift of seeing, remember? That's you!"

"You need to have faith, Mya."

"Faith in what? You know what… forget it. I personally think you have the wrong girl, or maybe your vision is wrong or something. All that mind erasing the Elders did to you could have jacked up your power… who knows."

"What are you saying Mya?"

"I'm saying NO! No way. Not in a million years. Noooooo thank you!!"

"Okay if that's how you really feel, then so be it," Michael said, not sounding surprised.

"Don't you care?" I asked, confused.

"Of course I care, but I already know how this ends. You have to figure this out on yo…" he stopped abruptly for a moment. "You have to go!"

"What? So that's it, you dump all this on me then send me away?"

"She's back! She can't find you down here," he replied frantically. "RUN! Three minutes!"

I raced up the stairs. When I reached the top, I locked the basement door and placed the coat rack in its original spot. I heard a loud thump coming from what sounded like the roof, and I froze, waiting to hear something else.

Chapter 22

"Nor?" I echoed.

Silence filled the house. The stairs creaked as I slowly placed one foot in front the other. I stood holding the railing for a moment to listen, nothing. I took out my phone to call Noreen and I heard her ringtone blaring from inside her room.

"Hey," Noreen answered on the second ring.

"Noreen, you're home?" I asked.

"Oh… yea, I came back for the car… my ride had to go somewhere."

"When did you get back?" I asked, reaching the top of the stairs.

"Two minutes ago maybe… why?"

I opened her bedroom door, and we hung up our phones.

"I didn't hear you come through the front," I said.

"Knock much? Sheesh!"

"My bad. But how did u get in here?" I asked, noticing the open window.

"The front door! Were you standing by the door waiting?" she replied defensively.

"Well, no, but…"

"Where were you Mya?"

Oh she's good, I thought to myself.

"Forget it," I chuckled.

"Great! We can go get our movie stuff now if you like."

"Yep. I'll grab my wallet."

"Perfect, and I'll meet you in the car."

Noreen could be difficult to manoeuvre around sometimes. I knew she hadn't come through the front door, but I had to stop pushing the issue because she was going to flip it on me. And her window being open… it was all too coincidental. Everywhere I turned, it seemed like people were keeping secrets but was I any better?

Later that evening, while I prepared our buttered popcorn and took our wine out the fridge, my phone buzzed with two text messages, one from Levi and the other from Sophia. I responded to Sophia first.

Sophia: Hey girl… you alive?
Mya: Yes I am! Just getting ready for a movie night with Noreen believe it or not
Sophia: WHAT? What did I miss??
Mya: Long story, I'll explain later.

Sophia: All right will I see you Monday at school? Missed you a few days last week.
Mya" Yep I'll be there for sure. How's Zohrah?
Sophia: She's good! She's the strong silent type
Mya: Good! Ok well I'll msg you later
Sophia: You better msg me later tonight so I know Noreen hasn't drugged you again!
Mya: LMAO don't worry I'm good

I put my phone down and received a call from Levi right after.

"Hey!"

"Hey I was just about to message you back," I replied.

"Oh that's cool. I just wanted to check in with you because the last time I saw you, you were in a mood."

"Oh yea… I try not to focus too much on that. I have so much going on right now," I said, remembering the dozens of people below me.

"Oh yea? Like what?"

"I'll tell you some other time," I smiled, loving that he was taking interest in me.

"Alright. Well, what are your plans for tonight?"

"I'm actually giving this sister thing a shot, and we're having a movie night."

"Wow… that's good. I think. Just be careful alright," he said, sounding a bit concerned. "But anyways, make sure to pencil me in this week. I can bring dinner and we can hang by your place."

"I'll check my schedule and get back to you," I replied playfully.

"Alright, well, enjoy your movie."

"I will, thanks."

I hang up as Noreen strolls into the kitchen.

"Mmm, down here smells so good! I love the smell of popcorn don't you? Who was that?" she asked.

"You don't know him."

"Him?"

"Here's the popcorn," I said, changing the subject. "I'll grab the wine and the glasses." I laughed while thinking to myself. Noreen would have to be damn near insane if she thought she was getting anywhere near my drink tonight!

That night we talked, laughed and filled up on popcorn, gummies and whatever else we found in the pantry. For those couple hours, it felt just like old times.

My alarm rang, waking me up earlier than I wanted. I lay in bed, wondering what day it was. Once it dawned on me that it was Monday, I contemplated if I really needed to get up for school. Since the world, as I knew it, blew up in my face, I'd had a hard time focusing in class. Every thought always diverted back to how much I wish things could go back to how they used to be when life was simple. However, since speaking to my Uncle Mike and seeing all those people suffering in that basement, it would be only natural that my lack of focus would intensify. Then there was Sophia; I couldn't help but feel guilty for dragging her into this mess. I constantly wondered what would have happened had I not invited her out for my birthday that night. What if I hadn't spoken to Zohrah that day in the hallway? Would we still be in this mess? I'd apologized several times to them both, but they didn't seem to understand why I felt responsible. They believed that things happened for a reason. However, I was grateful for them because I was not sure I would have survived any of this without Sophia or Zohrah by my side. I forced myself out of bed and threw on some clothes to try and get to school on time.

I got to school right when it was announced that my classes had been cancelled due to the absence of Mr. Henry. *Maybe he's gone to New York with Malachi?* I forced those thoughts from my mind; *I can't concern myself with this mess any more than I already have.* As I walked down the hall, I spotted Sophia and Zohrah's friendly faces. Zohrah looked amazing and back to her old self; she was totally healed. Since she'd started training on a daily basis, you could see the difference in her confidence. Her arms were toned and defined, and her posture was straight.

"You look amazing Z!" I said happily.

"Thanks," she replied shyly.

"Uh Hellooo, what am I, chopped liver?" Sophia chimed in.

"I don't think you need anyone to tell you what you already know," I smirked.

"True! You're right, carry on," Sophia giggled, making us all burst out laughing.

"How are things at home? How are you handling living with… you know?" Zohrah asked.

The vision of Sophia sitting on the floor with a gun pointed at her head trickled to the forefront of my subconscious.

"It has its days," I sighed.

"Did you ever find out what was behind that mysterious door you told us about?" Zohrah queried.

"Uh nope. Still looking," I lied.

"Okay, well, make sure to loop us in once you know," Sophia replied.

"Of course," I said, not making eye contact.

Just then, my phone buzzed with a text message from Levi:

Levi: Hey! Want some company tonight?
Mya: OMG yes I'd love that!
Levi: Alright, I'll bring dinner. What do you feel for?"
Mya: Jamaican food.
Levi: Bet. I'll msg you when I'm there.

"What's with the grin," Sophia questioned. "Let me guess, Levi!"

"We were just making plans for later. It's no big deal," I said, rolling my eyes. "What do you guys have planned for tonight," I asked, switching topics.

"Studying… nothing exciting," Zohrah replied.

"Same here… nothing," Sophia answered.

"When things settle down, we should definitely go out to dinner or something."

We all agree to make plans and go our separate ways. I send Phillip a quick text letting him know to pick me up.

Around 7p.m I received a message from Levi saying he was outside. I rushed downstairs to open the front door. I inhaled his scent from his sweater as he pulled me in for a tight hug. I did not want to let go. He smiled brightly while I placed his jacket and shoes in the front closet. I haven't had anyone over since moving in with Malachi. And since Malachi thought it was a good idea to come home early to "surprise" us, I was a bit nervous to see how this evening would play out. I led him down the corridor to where the kitchen was; Levi and I entered, holding two paper bags. We placed the bags on the counter; Malachi was sitting at the table typing on his laptop.

"Hey uh... this is Levi. Levi, this is Malachi, my father," I said, praying this introduction would be short.

They shook hands. Levi flinched slightly, and I knew he felt Malachi's power surge through him.

"Nice to meet you sir," Levi said, releasing his grip from the handshake.

"Likewise," replied Malachi.

Noreen ran downstairs.

"I heard the door open. Is someone here? Ouu I smell food," she said but stopped in her tracks once she noticed Levi and squints.

Levi looked up, but once he saw her face, his smile faded, and his eyes opened wide with recognition.

"This is my sister Noreen," I introduced them while watching their strange reactions.

"Have we met before?" asked Noreen.

"Briefly," Levi replied as he recalled the electricity he felt when they bumped into each other that night.

We stood in silence for a few minutes.

"Okay! Well, Levi is going to hang with me for a bit if that's cool with you. He brought food, and from the looks of it, there's enough for everyone to have some," I said, eyeing the takeout containers as he took them out of the bags.

"Yea help yourselves," he offered.

"After we eat we'll be in my room if you need me," I said.

That caught Malachi's attention immediately as he looked at me with concern.

"I'm sorry?" Malachi asked.

"Oh come on! Don't act like such a 'dad'," I responded, rolling my eyes.

"But I am your dad," he retorted.

"Yea, but as of like last week… you can't just come and expect things t…"

"Yea relax, Dad. Don't be annoying," Noreen interjected while grabbing a plate.

"Fine! I won't be 'annoying' just keep the door open. Is that too much to ask?"

"Fine," I replied, relieved.

We all dig in. Surprisingly, the evening went by without any hiccups. Malachi and Levi seemed to actually get along, which was insane when you think about it. Couple months ago, Malachi was counting sheep on the cement because of Levi. Of course he doesn't know that, but it was strange nonetheless.

As soon as we entered my room, he sat on my chair, and I reached for the remote and turned on the television.

"Is that a PS5?" Levi asked, standing to get a closer look.

"Huh? Uh yea I think so," I answered, not really listening. "Sooo… you knew Noreen? What's that about?"

"Oh… uh yea. That's a long story," he replied.

"I've got time," I said, sitting across from him.

Levi explained the night he saw her and the power he felt from her. I listened intently and asked questions. I remembered the conversation with Noreen where I asked her what other ability she possessed, and she said just that one. Then I remembered her being in her room when she didn't use the front door and her window was open.

I set those thoughts aside. Levi and I laughed and talked for a few hours, losing track of the time. Around 1 A.M, I walked Levi to his car.

"Thanks for coming and being so nice to Malachi," I said. "I know that wasn't easy."

"I knew it's something you'd want… I just thought I'd be the mature one," he said, leaning against his car.

"Is that right?" I smiled, stepping closer to him. "You know me that well now?" I replied playfully.

Levi matched my step, and by that time, we were so close I could feel the heat radiating off his lips. Unable to resist the undeniable attraction, Levi reached for my neck and jawline with his hand. I leaned my head back, allowing myself to submit to his kiss. He held the small of my back, pulling me in, and I wrapped my arms around his neck.

Chapter 23

Falling asleep was difficult because I kept replaying the kiss Levi and I shared, but when I finally started to doze off, I heard rustling and whispers outside my bedroom door. I listened for a moment, and nothing; I closed my eyes, assuming I was hearing things, until I heard loud whispers. I sat up in bed, and I saw shadows appear under my door. I threw my comforter off my legs and crept towards the whispers; I pushed my ear against the cool door to get a better listen. It was Noreen and Malachi; it sounded like they were disagreeing about something but I couldn't make out what they were saying. The whispers started to become further away, they must have been on the move. Once I couldn't hear them anymore, I cracked my door open to see the back of Noreen's head going down the stairs. Once they disappeared from my view, I quietly tiptoed to the stairs and peered over the railing to see where they were exactly. I heard the sound of a door being unlocked, so I snuck down the stairs, trying not to make a sound. I held my breath with each step I took, hoping that the stairs wouldn't creak under my weight. I followed their murmurs of anger and irritation to the bottom of the stairs, but when I got there, the foyer was empty. Where did they go? It was then I noticed the coat rack was moved, and the basement door was open. I stood at the top of the stairs leading to the basement, pondering if I should go down or wait. The sudden whaling and cries startled me, and I struggled not to race down there and stop whatever was happening.

"SHUTUP… All of you!" Malachi boomed.

"You don't have to do this," said a familiar voice that sounded like Uncle Mike.

I felt my heart sink into my stomach.

"Yea Dad… we don't have to do this. We have to let these people go!" Noreen tried to reason.

"You and…. You, come here," Malachi demanded, ignoring his brother and daughter.

"No… please, I just want to go home," a woman sobbed. "I won't tell a soul about any of this just… please let us go."

Everyone joined in with their cries and shrieks, begging for their freedom.

"EVERYBODY KEEP QUIET!" Malachi yelled, and instantly, the room became silent. "Now, you two stand up," Malachi said calmly.

"Dad come on…" Noreen started again.

"Don't give me that Noreen! You're no saint… why on earth would you want *him* to be free to tell everyone wha… ahhh. It's all becoming clear now," he said.

"Dad please," she pleaded.

"You think he'll forgive you after all of this? You think things will just go back to how it was once this is over? Noreen, let me give you a dose of reality. He will NEVER forgive you. Not now, not ever," he said firmly.

There was silence.

"You know what to do with her," Malachi said.

I breathed heavily, gripping the door as anger rose up within me. *Let them go, Dad, please, you can do better; BE better*, I whispered to myself. Should I have intervened and put a stop to this insanity? It's already known I couldn't battle my father on my own, but how could I stand there and listen to this happen and not help those innocent people? The sound of agony rang from below, and it hit me in my gut. The screams echoed in my ears, and I saw flashbacks of Zohrah being held in the air as she kicked and choked. Her body shrunk as Malachi sucked the life out of her. Then, a second voice shouted in torment. I covered my ears, but no matter how hard I squeezed, the sounds of these people were imprinted in my mind. I couldn't take it anymore.

I ran upstairs to get away from it all. I slammed my bedroom door and jumped on my bed, pulling the cover up to my chin. I don't know why I thought I could change that man. Any feeling of progress and positivity melted away and was replaced with disappointment and agony. When I realized just how much I must have saddened Uncle Mike by refusing to help take down my father, tears filled my eyes. I cried myself to sleep.

I woke up to total darkness and checked the time: 4:50 A.M. I began to feel nauseous as I recalled what had taken place hours prior. The thought of Malachi going down there and undertaking this terrible act to innocent people was revolting. But to then force Noreen, his flesh and blood to participate against her will. That was mind-blowing, to say the least. I can't force him to change; he has to want to do that for himself. I got up and washed my tear-stained face. I stare at myself in the mirror, battling with the thoughts that kept surfacing in my cognizance. Every deliberation I went through mentally had one common denominator. This has to end.

I dried my face and grabbed my copy of the key before heading outside my room. I glanced down the hall to ensure Malachi and Noreen's bedroom doors were closed. I carefully walked down the stairs, unlocked the door quietly and closed it behind me. When I reached the bottom, I felt around for the string hanging from the bulb. When the light was turned on, everyone jumped in fear. I stared at them, and I could see the scarcity of hope and faith in their eyes. I could see that they believed this was their destiny. They believed they were going to die here in this basement and never see their loved ones again. Some had bloodshot eyes like they hadn't stopped crying, while others had dark circles under their eyes, showing they hadn't slept in days. I saw two limp bodies lying on a blanket in the corner, looking elderly and delicate. Malachi and Noreen stripped them of their powers and then left them to fend for themselves. Suddenly, Uncle Mike stood before me.

"This can't continue," I said, scanning the area.

"I know."

"You saw this coming?" I asked, finally making eye contact.

"Yes I did."

"Why didn't you tell me so I could stop it?" I asked, frustrated.

"You needed to hear it for yourself. I had to allow it to play out for itself so you could come to the truth on your own."

"And what's that?"

"You already know the truth. Now the question is, what will you do about it?"

I took a moment to glance around at everyone there.

"I can't turn a blind eye to what I witnessed tonight," I acknowledged. "I know I didn't want to be forced into this, but I've realized this isn't about me; it's about all of us. So what happens now?" I asked.

"That's up to you Mya. I should be asking you that question," he answered.

I began to weigh my options in my mind. *Yes my life will change but change is good, change is inevitable. Is this something I'm ready for? Was everything I've been through in my life thus far preparation for what's to come next? I'm not sure if I'm ready or if I ever will be, mentally at least. I will have to train physically and develop my abilities to be stronger and have more control. I can try and talk myself out of this all day but I know what needs to be done.*

I was so deep in thought I didn't hear ankle chains dragging closer as someone cautiously eavesdropped while Uncle Mike and I conversed.

"Where do we begin?" I asked.

"You won't be able to do to is alone. This is a big mission that will take months of preparation and planning. Do you know anyone who would be willing to help, people you trust?" he asked.

"Excuse me," a quiet voice interrupted us.

"Yes?" I asked.

"Are you Mya? I mean the Mya?" the young man asked.

"Uh…yea," I replied, looking at Uncle Mike.

"I couldn't help but overhear you talking with Michael, and I want to help you… in any way I can."

Michael and I looked at each other and considered his request. He looked beat up and worn out. His clothes were frayed and old, just like everyone else down here. I could see a long scar along his cheek on the right side of his face. I stared at him to see if I would recognize him, but with his dishevelled hair around his face and unkempt beard, he was barely identifiable. Who was this mystery man that wanted to help us? Although he seemed weary, his dark eyes had a passion and fire that I hadn't witnessed in anyone since coming down here. He had something to prove, and I know Uncle Mike saw it too. This wasn't just some suicide mission for him; this was personal! The young man stood waiting patiently while we deliberated on what we should do. Uncle Mike was the first to respond.

"Alright son, what's your name?"

He lifted his head and looked at us.

"Daniel… my name is Daniel…"